NUMBER THREE ★ GHOST TOWN

GHOSTOWNERS

SHANIKO
SCHOOL

DIST. 67

Shadow of Shaniko

BY CALAMITY JAN

For Ana and Maya — ♡ Calamity Jan

For information contact:

WildWest Publishing
P O Box 11658
Olympia, WA 98508

Printed in the United States of America
by Gorham Printing, Rochester, Washington
Cover and book design by Kathy Campbell
Cover and text photographs by Jan Pierson

Second WildWest Printing 2004

ISBN: 0-9721800-2-8

LCCN: 2002110775

http://www.calamityjan.com
http://www.booksinprint.com/php/phpFeaturedTitle.asp?WildWest_Publishing

Dedicated to Michal Paige and Gabe,
two cool characters in this story—
and in real life, too.

Contents

CHAPTER 1

The Howling

Meggie Bryson heard the freaky howling shortly after midnight. She grabbed her sheet and froze like a stick of deadwood lying on the desert floor. "Pa—Paige?" she whispered, trying not to wake her aunt in the van just outside their tent. "Paige—did you hear that?"

Her best friend snorted and rolled over.

"Paige, wake up!" Meggie said hoarsely, yanking her sheet. Dark blonde hair fell like sage grass in the pale, quivering light coming through the tent. *"There's something howling out there!"*

Paige Morefield shot up, slamming her head on the lantern hanging overhead. "Owww!"

"Shhh!" Meggie whispered again.

Twelve-year-old Paige Morefield rubbed her head, then her eyes. But they were open wide now—as round and wide as the moon hovering over this ghost town in central eastern Oregon. She was listening.

"Listen. There it goes again..." Meggie swallowed each word carefully, wondering if maybe they ought to wake up Aunt Abby. "It's getting louder, Paige. Closer."

"Probably a coyote," Paige mumbled, diving back down into her pillow. "Now let me sleep. It's our vacation, remember?"

"No, Paige. I know the difference. That is not a coyote. That is *definitely* not a coyote." Meggie's wide blue eyes peered out through the small, screened window of the tent and stared into the moonlit darkness. Sagebrush crawled across the high bunchgrass flat like huge, dark spiders. She felt an eerie chill.

Paige inched up beside Meggie, rubbing her aching head. "This better be worth the stupid lump I just got on my skull."

Meggie sighed and watched Paige press her small nose flat against the window screen. Her best friend acted like this was the friendly neighborhood coyote sitting on some porch. Had she forgotten that Shaniko was a *ghost* town, for crying out loud? *Geee.*

"Whoa, hey—wait a minute! I think I hear it!" Wide brown eyes caught the reflection of the moon.

"I told you, Paige." Meggie groped for her glasses, then slipped them on, pressing her nose against the screen. But it was too dark to see much of anything except those weird sagebrush spiders crawling under the moon.

They both waited. And listened.

"It sounds like it's coming from that old school," Meggie said.

"How's a coyote supposed to get into the school when it's boarded up?"

"Paige, that's not a coyote." Meggie turned to her best friend like she'd lost her brain.

"You swear it's not?"

"I don't have to swear, Paige. Coyotes do this little 'yap-yap-yap'—*then* the howl. This howling is totally different. Look, we've been hanging around ghost towns long enough to know the difference between a coyote and a..."

"A *what*?" Paige faced Meggie.

Meggie drew a deep breath. "I'm not sure."

Paige backed off, her eyes still holding Meggie's gaze. "Okay, then we'll find out, Meggie. We'll check out that school in the morning."

"But it's boarded up, remember?" Meggie reminded her. They had scoped out the place when they first arrived and set up camp at the edge of town a few days before. "I think the Shaniko School shut down when the town did."

Paige nodded. "It's probably even older than your aunt. Doesn't it say 1902 right under the bell tower?"

Meggie couldn't remember the date exactly, but if Paige was right, then the school had to be at least a hundred years old. "Yeah, well it's a *lot* older than Aunt Abby, Paige," she said quietly. Even though her aunt was in her forties, which was fairly old, at least she wasn't falling apart like that school.

"But," Paige added, "just because it's boarded up doesn't mean we can't get in, does it?" Her eyes flashed once more in the pale shaft of moonlight creeping through the screened window of the tent.

Meggie gazed at her best friend who always seemed to think of ways to overcome obstacles. Even though they were both twelve and Paige was smaller, Paige Morefield was always the one to step out and face the danger first. Paige was a combination of Wonder Woman, Batman and Godzilla in a size five pair of Reeboks.

"We'll check it out in the morning," Paige went on with strength and boldness in her voice. "I've been wanting to get into that old place, anyway."

Meggie took off her glasses and lay back down on her sleeping bag, pulling up her sheet. She felt the same way. *And why not?* Now that 'Shaniko Days' was over, they could probably get into that school without anybody seeing them. Shaniko Days had been fun, though, with the old-time parade and stagecoaches and covered wagons. She and Paige even bought some souvenirs. But there were too many people walking around to do much exploring, so that's why they were glad when most of the people packed up their booths and left town. And when Aunt Abby told them her digging permit extended a few more days—they practically melted with joy.

Having an aunt who was an archaeologist was definitely more fun than having the ordinary type who baked cookies and shopped at malls. Meggie's aunt was *so* cool. Meggie figured Aunt Abby probably never baked a cookie in her whole life. And when she went shopping, it was mostly to get supplies for the next ghost town dig. These ghost town getaways were like heaven on earth and Meggie knew that she and Paige were probably the luckiest sixth graders in the town of Trout Lake.

Every summer when Aunt Abby hitched her rickety trailer to the van and took them off to some ghost town in the western United States, it was like they were driving backwards into time. Back to dusty, forgotten old towns that were like dry bones just waiting to come back to life...

Dry bones waiting to come back to life.

Meggie pulled the sheet up tighter around her neck, her thoughts shifting back to the weird howling. But it had stopped now, hadn't it? But why? she wondered. Well, they'd just have to find out for themselves.

It wasn't going to be easy getting into that school, she realized, remembering the padlock on the old door in front. *Unless we find some loose boards or a door that might be ready to fall off its hinges.* Meggie muffled a giggle, knowing that with Paige along, there was a strong possibility that might happen.

Then, just before she closed her eyes and drifted off to sleep, she heard it again.

Eerie.

Mournful.

Wailing like a ghost in the dusty Shaniko wind....

Shaniko School

CHAPTER 2

School Daze

Aunt Abby left the campsite before sun-up the next morning, leaving a note.

"She says she's gonna be digging for artifacts at a site west of town and that she'll be back by dinner," Meggie told Paige. "Also that we're supposed to stay out of trouble because it would take too long for Rescue 911 or the Swat Team to get here."

Paige tucked her shirt into her cutoffs and grinned. "When she starts talking like that, I'm glad she's *your* aunt and not mine." She sat down at the portable camp table, finishing an apple.

"Come on, Paige," Meggie grinned back, sitting down beside her. "She's got a point."

Paige poured some dry cereal into her hand and began eating. "She does?"

"Well, if we get in trouble or something, what would we do? I mean, isn't Burntoven the nearest town? Or, Cross Hollows or maybe Hay Creek Valley? Can't you just hear it, Paige? 'Hello? Is this Burntoven? We have a child who has fallen into a pit and is being stung by scorpions. Can you please send out the next medical team as soon as possible'?" She took some dry cereal and began munching.

"I think Burntoven is a ghost town, Meggie."

"I *know*, Paige."

After breakfast, they cleaned up and locked up the storage trailer.

"Well, there probably won't be that many scorpions crawling around in the school, anyhow," Paige said, hitching up her backpack.

Meggie drew a sharp breath.

"And since Aunt Abby left before we did, then I guess we can't ask her permission about getting in there, either, can we?" Paige went on. She didn't seem sad.

Meggie hesitated. "I guess we *could* get permission from those people who run the hotel, though." She grabbed the box of cereal.

"Let's not bother them. They're probably too tired out after 'Shaniko Days,' don't you think?"

Meggie agreed completely.

She and Paige left the campsite and headed up the main street toward the school on the far edge of town, still munching on the cereal snack. Even though Meggie knew there were only a handful of people living around Shaniko, she didn't want it to look as though they were snooping or breaking and entering. Aunt Abby had taught them to respect the buildings and any artifacts they might find. Most people didn't understand that, though, and so she and Paige had made a silent pact to do all their exploring and detective work undercover.

Keeping alert, they walked along the boardwalk, passing the antique car museum and a wagon yard with some buckboards and farm machinery lying around. The vacant City Hall and fire bell tower lined one side of the street, and on their left were a few tourist shops and the

Shaniko Hotel and Café. They crossed the two-lane highway behind the hotel, moving quietly toward the school. Highway 97 seemed more like a country road, which was a good thing. *The fewer the cars—the less chance we're going to be seen*, Meggie knew, gazing around at the shacks dotting the outskirts of town.

"I wonder how Shaniko got its name?" She turned to Paige. "I never heard such a weird name in my life, have you? Except maybe Burntoven. Yeah, Burntoven is pretty weird, too." Meggie munched her cereal absently.

"Aunt Abby said the town was named after this guy and his wife who came from Germany. Their name was Scher—neckau or something like that."

Meggie paused, remembering. "Oh yeah, that's right. Didn't she say that nobody, including the Indians, could pronounce it, so that's why they just called it Shaniko?"

Paige shrugged, watching a rabbit dart under the broken-down fence surrounding the school.

Meggie knelt down beside her and fingered some huge brass rings attached to the ground on either side of the gatepost.

"What're those?"

"I'm not sure," Meggie replied, "but I think maybe they were for tying up the horses. Yeah, maybe the kids got to ride their horses to school."

"Cool!" Paige laughed. "A lot more fun than those lame yellow busses we have to ride in, that's for sure."

"Just picture it, Paige. Picture us galloping down Highway 141 past the Grange and General Store, then hitching up our horses right in front of the Trout Lake School. Wouldn't that be an absolute blast?"

Paige nodded, standing up and gazing around, her short hair shivering in the breeze. "Too bad we didn't live here in Shaniko a hundred years ago. It would have been so cool coming here to school, don't you think?"

Meggie agreed.

"I really like this place, Meggie. This old school isn't one bit spooky in broad daylight. It doesn't scare me *at all*."

"It doesn't scare me either." Meggie had already pushed the howling and ghost thoughts out of her mind completely. Glancing behind them to make sure the coast was still clear, she turned and walked up to the old building. *I hope it doesn't collapse on our heads, though. It is old.*

"It says Shaniko School District 67," Paige went on, stepping carefully along the rotting boardwalk and glancing up at the empty bell tower that formed a peak just above the eight-sided entrance. Her sun-bronzed face squinted in the glare of the morning sun. A padlock hung on the old door in the encased porch below. "Yeah, this school is definitely older than Aunt Abby."

Meggie walked up the steps to see if the padlock or door might be ajar. But no such luck. "Too bad," she said to Paige.

"Hey. Wait a minute! " Paige called from behind. "I think we're in luck!"

Meggie backed down the steps.

"Will you look at that?" Paige stood at the foot of the steps and pointed to a small window just to their right. "No glass, Meggie. Not even boarded up."

Yesss.

"And will you also cast your eyes on this convenient little roof right here below the window, Megan Bryson?" Paige pointed to a cellar door, framed by a small, low roof. "Pretty cool, huh?"

"Way to go, Shaniko!" Meggie laughed, racing over beside her. "Here, let me help you up!" She secured her box of cereal under one arm, glancing over her shoulder one more time. Except for a car passing by on the road across the field, there was nothing—nothing but grasshoppers and rabbits and a few noisy magpies. Bending over, Meggie locked her arms together, giving Paige a foothold. "Okay, one—two—three—UP!"

Paige almost flew onto the roof, then reached for Meggie and pulled her up.

Meggie caught her balance, watching Paige squeeze through the window like a little brown lizard in sneakers.

"Hey!" Paige called back. "This is so cool, Meggie!"

Meggie squeezed her lanky frame inside and gazed around at the huge room piled with junk. Brushing the dust off her cutoffs, she stared at the old boards and desks and benches lying around like bones. It must have been a classroom once, she realized. Or maybe the gym? Meggie brushed her hair out of her face, then followed Paige into the next larger room. This room looked as though it had once been divided into two classrooms. "Maybe this was a three-room schoolhouse," she suggested. "A Little-House-on-the-Prairie type school, don't you think?"

Paige tossed her hair out of her eyes in a quick gesture. "Yeah. It would've been awesome going to school here," she said, walking into the next room. "Kids probably snuck up in that tower or chased lizards during recess instead of going to the library and stuff like that."

Meggie agreed, glancing at a few desks and boards and junk scattered around. A tall, round heating stove stood like a guard in one corner, WATERBURY SPECIAL FURNACE embossed on its now-rusty door. Even a lopsided blackboard stared with a blank, gray face. No chalk. No more assignments. Meggie realized that the kids who used to sit in these desks were probably old by now. Maybe even in the graveyard.

She pushed the uneasy thoughts aside and turned to her friend, wondering if maybe they were intruding. "Paige, do you..."

But before she could finish, a sudden crack—then a thud—broke into her words and split the air. Meggie grabbed Paige, her heart falling like a rock.

They were not alone.

Old Furnace

CHAPTER 3

Ghostly Warning

"Eeeeyowww!" Paige whirled around and raced toward the window. Meggie followed, breakfast cereal, cobwebs and dust flying,

They hit the cellar roof, then the ground like two speeding bullets.

Meggie raced through the gate, skidding to a sudden halt. "It—there was..." Meggie couldn't finish. The words were stuck like sawdust in her throat.

"Yeah," Paige nodded, holding on to a fence post like it was her only hope. "Yeah, well—well there's some—one in there, that's for sure!"

Or something Meggie realized. But Paige must have known what she was thinking because her face had turned as pale as ashes.

"A ghost?" Paige exploded, nearly knocking Meggie over with her words.

"No!" Meggie shot back, tossing her blonde hair from her wide blue eyes. "No. No, Paige! There aren't any ghosts in ghost towns! Aunt Abby's been exploring ghost towns for years, and she's never *ever* seen one, remember? She's got tons of college degrees. She knows!"

"Right," Paige agreed, beginning to relax. "A coyote probably got into the school and got spooked when we came in."

"Coyote?" Meggie caught her breath, then gazed across the yellow sage and bunchgrass at the old building with a witch-hat tower.

"Yeah, last night I told you, Meggie. I told you it was probably just a coyote," Paige went on, brushing the dust off her arms and starting back toward the school. "Poor little thing. We probably scared it to death. When it heard us it probably knocked over a board trying to get out."

Meggie drew back and watched her best friend walk back into that—that *trap*. She was doing it again—maybe facing death and acting like it was recess and she forgot her jacket. "Paige! Paige Morefield!" Meggie's words spilled out like her ill-fated box of cereal. "Where are you going?"

"Back into that school, where else?" Paige called over her shoulder.

"Excuse me?"

"I said I'm going back into the school, Meggie."

"Yeah. Right. Straight into the trap."

"Huh?" Paige paused and turned, squinting against the bright morning sun.

"How can you be one-hundred percent sure that was a coyote?"

Paige frowned. "What else?"

Meggie licked her dry lips and tried to get the words out, but they wouldn't come. *It couldn't be a ghost, could it? No. Okay, maybe not a ghost. But what could it be? Something was in that school.*

"Maybe it was a big lizard," Paige cut into her muddled thoughts like she was reading her mind. "Yeah, I'll bet anything that's what it was. Lizards zoom around all over this place."

Meggie wanted to believe that with all her heart, but the lizard wasn't any better than the coyote. She began backing up slowly. "I never heard of a lizard that howls."

"I haven't either," Paige replied, turning and following Meggie back toward town.

"The howling throws everything off."

"Yeah."

"We've got a heavy-duty mystery here, Paige."

Paige nodded, her short, dark hair rippling in the warm wind.

"But we can't just let a mystery go unsolved, can we? No matter how dangerous. No matter how scary." Meggie's heart thumped like an Indian drum, but she felt a whole lot safer now that there was enough distance between them and the school.

"No. We can't," Paige agreed. "We just can't leave this thing up in the air."

"We are the best ghost town detectives in the West, Paige. The best."

A magpie screeched from a rooftop overhead and Paige nearly fell over backwards.

"Okay, then let's go back," Meggie paused and turned around, facing the school once more.

"Whaa...?"

"Yes. Yes, we go back," Meggie replied, keeping her voice and her tall, slender frame steady and sure. *I can't believe I'm saying this. Feeling this way.* The tables were turning and Meggie wondered if it had been 'Shaniko Days' that had inspired her. Yes, that must have been it. The parade. The cowboys and Indians and stagecoaches and covered wagons made her think of their brave ancestors who had defied the elements and made history. If the pioneers of Shaniko could face the dangers of the unknown, then why couldn't they? The bright blue sky caught the clear color and sense of purpose in her eyes.

"You don't think this town was dangerous like Nighthawk or Bodie, do you?" Paige asked quietly.

Meggie drew a deep breath. "I'm not sure since there wasn't a gold rush or anything like that in Shaniko, but there was a big gold strike at Canyon City."

"Canyon City is pretty close to Shaniko," Paige put in.

"I know, but when that gold was gone, people just got land and sheep and built their houses and stuff like that. The ghost town book I read said that central Oregon, including Shaniko, was just one big sheep ranch back then. No, I don't think it was dangerous here."

"Wait a minute. What about the Indians, Meggie? If there wasn't anything dangerous going on around Shaniko, how come there were Indians attacking the Shaniko Stage Line during the parade yesterday? Why would they do wild stuff like that if it hadn't actually happened?"

Paige had a point, Meggie realized. Maybe the town was dangerous once, but that was then and this is now. "That crazy stuff happened a hundred years ago. Besides, those Indians in the parade weren't for real."

"Weren't for real? Hello?" Paige threw out her small chin and faced Meggie. "In case you didn't notice, those were one-hundred percent authentic Native American Indians on those horses. Didn't you see those tomahawks and that long black hair flying around? And those weird feather hats? People *do not* get those feather hats at Wal-Mart, Meggie."

Meggie realized her friend might be right.

Paige tucked her shirt into her cutoffs. "You don't think Indians do stuff like that now, do you?"

"What do you mean?"

"Do you think they'd ever attack our tent?"

"Huh?"

"The tent. Or Aunt Abby's van."

"No way. Not with Aunt Abby inside."

Paige sighed. "You're probably right. Anyhow, I don't think we have to worry. There are some Native Americans in Trout Lake and they're *really* nice. They're not wild or anything. Andrea Framebinder is a cheerleader and John Scott..."

"Wait a minute," Meggie said. "How'd we get off the subject?"

"Huh?"

"We were talking about the ghost or lizard, or whatever-it-is in that school. How did the Indians get into this?"

"I don't know," Paige said, cutting across the main street and heading around behind the City Hall and bell tower. "Well, it was probably just a big lizard in that school, anyhow. I don't think we have a thing to worry about. Not a thing."

Meggie rolled her eyes heavenward. "So now it's a lizard?"

"Or maybe a rattlesnake," Paige went on, brushing dust and cobwebs off her arms. "I hear they're crawling all over this place. Or a bull snake."

"Bull snake?"

You know those huge yellow and brown things? They are actually thicker than my arm." Paige held out her small sun-bronzed arm.

"Paige, cut it out."

"Actually, if we had to choose, I'd choose a bull snake over a rattler, though, wouldn't you, Meggie? Rattlesnakes are poisonous and without 911 we'd probably be dead in ten minutes." Paige turned to her friend who had slowed down to a complete stop. "Meggie?"

The black magpie screamed again and Meggie nearly fell over backwards.

"What's wrong?"

"Cool it, Paige, okay? Let's just face what we have to face when we have to face it." Meggie could hardly hear her own words over the thumping inside her t-shirt. Between the magpie and Paige, she could've had heart failure right there in front of the Pioneer Saloon. They had enough danger staring them in the face without Paige throwing in snakes.

"Yeah, sure. Okay." Paige tossed her hair out of her brown eyes and shrugged.

This time Meggie took the lead, crossing a side street and cutting behind some old buildings with false fronts and peeling paint. Checking to make sure the coast was clear, they crossed the road and entered the school grounds once more. Meggie forced the black thoughts out of her head and felt her newfound strength returning. *We are first and foremost ghostowners. We have a mystery to solve.*

She drew a deep breath, then motioned for Paige to give her a hand on to the cellar roof. *Hey, no problem. I'll go in first. Nothing's in there. Nothing at all.* She slipped her sunglasses into the back pocket of her cutoffs, crawling through the splintery window frame. *Maybe just a box fell off a shelf. Sure. I'll bet that was it. But if it wasn't a box, then— then we'll find out what it was.* She smiled inwardly at the strength— the boldness coursing through her veins.

In seconds they were inside the dimly lit school, gazing around in the eerie silence. Paige started to speak, but Meggie motioned her quiet. She slipped on her glasses and started toward the hall, wishing the old boards underneath her feet would quit creaking so loud. They hadn't explored the back part of the school yet.

"I've never seen so much junk in my life," Paige whispered, gazing around in the shadows.

"Yeah, even worse than my little brother's room," Meggie whispered back, leading the way into a room with weird fixtures hanging sideways on the slatted wooden wall. Some old toilets were lying around on the rotting floorboards.

"Oooops," Paige giggled. "I think we're in the boys bathroom."

Meggie stopped in her tracks, staring at the peeling white paint and primitive fixtures lying upside down. An old toilet seat stared up like a big white eye. "Yuck," she grimaced, backing up.

Paige had already backed out, heading towards the girl's bathroom. "This one's just as gross," she whispered over her shoulder.

Meggie agreed. Nothing but junk back here. She turned and hurried past the cloakroom and up the hall toward the classrooms. "Maybe we'll find a clue or something out here," she muttered. "Tracks in the dust, maybe."

But before Paige caught up with her, Meggie had stopped dead in her tracks.

"What's the matter?" Paige blurted, skidding to a halt.

Meggie couldn't speak. She couldn't breathe. Terror nailed her feet to the floor as she stared at the blackboard in disbelief.

The lopsided thing no longer stared down with a gray, blank face. Chalk-white words spelled out the warning:

GET OUT!

CHAPTER 4

The Ghost of Shaniko?

Meggie and Paige made it back to the campsite in less than three minutes.

"I—I just can't believe it!" Meggie said when she finally caught her breath and could talk without choking. "Somebody *was* in that school! And whoever it is, he's leaving messages!" Frantically, she unzipped the tent, diving inside.

Paige was on her heels, her eyes almost as wide as those toilet seats lying back in that old bathroom. Hands trembling, she zipped the flap behind them.

"He was warning us, Paige."

Her best friend nodded again, breathing hard, staring wide-eyed. "No—not a *he*, Meggie. I don't think it was a person."

Meggie swallowed hard, wondering if Paige might be right. "Not a lizard or coyote, *that's* for sure," she said, wiping a nervous sweat off her face.

"Yeah. They can't spell. At least I never met a coyote that smart."

"Wait a minute, Paige..."

"But do you think ghosts can?" Paige went on. "Could a ghost just pick up the chalk and write like that? I mean, don't they just float around and walk through walls and blackboards and stuff like that?"

A ghost? No. It couldn't be. Meggie ran her fingers through her long, straight hair, still trying to clear her head. *Or could it? Could Aunt Abby be wrong this time?* she wondered, bracing herself against the wall. She hoped her aunt had the facts about ghosts, but if she didn't and that school was haunted, then they'd better find out now. This little adventure might be leading to something a whole lot more serious than coyotes howling in the wind.

"Let's ask Harriet over at the Shaniko Café," Paige said. "She's probably been around for a long time. Maybe she'll know if Shaniko has ghosts. Maybe she'll have some facts."

Meggie agreed, knotting her hair into a ponytail with a nervous twist. They each ate a sandwich, then zipped the tent back up and walked up the street toward the Shaniko Hotel and Café. The two-story brick building looked to Meggie as though nothing could ever destroy it. She remembered Aunt Abby telling her and Paige that the hotel had been built around the turn of the century and that it had survived the big fire of 1903—the same year a deadly smallpox epidemic struck Shaniko.

They walked through the hotel lobby with its threadbare furniture, then into the café. "Did you know the Shaniko Hotel used to be called the Columbia Southern Hotel and was really ritzy in its day?" she said to Paige.

Paige shook her head. She seemed to be more interested in getting something to drink at the moment and Meggie could hardly blame her. It *was* getting hot.

Paige ordered two sodas and took them out under the shaded porch supported by white painted columns.

"Uh, Harriet? Have you got a minute?" Meggie asked, motioning the waitress over. Paige moved aside, making room at the table.

"Sure, honey," the woman replied, wiping her damp hands on her apron. "Not too busy now that Shaniko Days are over." She pulled up an empty whiskey barrel and sat down beside the girls.

"Does Shaniko have ghosts?" Paige blurted.

The carefully groomed woman brushed a wisp of brown hair from her damp forehead and leaned closer. "*Whaat?*"

"Are their ghosts hanging around this place?" It was Meggie now. They might as well face this head on.

Harriet smiled and shook her head. "No, girls. No ghosts."

"But we..."

Meggie cut into Paige's words. "We—wondered, that's all," she said quickly. "Thanks a lot, Harriet. Sure is a hot day, huh?"

"But, Meggie," Paige said, grabbing her arm, "what about the school?"

Meggie silenced Paige with a sharp glance.

"The school?" Harriet lowered her thin, finely plucked eyebrows. She wasn't smiling now.

"Uh, oh yes, right. The school. The school is sooo cool! We *love* old schools and buildings. That Pioneer Saloon is awesome, too, isn't it Paige?" Meggie turned so fast her ponytail slapped her in the face. "We are *definitely* finding fun things to do around this place!"

Harriet's hooded eyes narrowed to slits.

"Uh, yeah. That's right." Paige stood up stiffly, forcing a smile. "Say, Meggie—why don't we check out the graveyard and see if we can find some old coins and stuff like that lying around. Or bones. Whatever."

"Yeah, good idea!" Meggie drank the last of her pop and stood up quickly, pushing her chair back. She turned to Harriet. "Uh, weren't the old coins called Allies or something like that?"

"Yes," Harriet replied, her unsmiling gaze lingering on Meggie. "But you can't get into the graveyard now. It's on private property. And no digging around for coins, either. Your aunt is the only one with a permit to gather artifacts."

"Oh, sure, well—not a problem. It doesn't take a graveyard to keep us occupied," Meggie said, her smile as tight as wire. She wanted to get away from this woman. They both did. "Uh, weren't Allies worth something like fifty cents back then?" she muttered absently.

Harriet nodded stiffly.

"Yeah. Well, 'bye Harriet," Paige said, backing up.

The waitress didn't answer. She turned abruptly, walking back into the restaurant at a brisk pace.

"What's wrong with her?" Paige said as soon as they were out of sight of the hotel.

"I think she knows something, Paige. I think she's keeping something from us."

"Whoa! Our second clue maybe?"

Meggie hesitated. "No, our third."

"Third?" Paige searched her face.

"The first clue was the howling," Meggie said, keeping her voice low. "The second was the warning on the blackboard."

"Oh yeah, and the third might be Harriet who knows something we don't know."

Meggie nodded and drew a deep breath. *Exactly. But what? What does Harriet know?* "We have to go back there, Paige. We have to go back to that school and find out what's going on. Why does she or...*someone* want us to stay out of there?"

Paige wrapped her arms around her small frame and shivered in the ninety-degree heat. "We *could* go back to the campsite and read or listen to the radio. Or maybe we could go looking for some of those old coins—those Allies. Without digging, of course." Her dark eyes flashed.

"Paige," Meggie said, "we both know it's against the law to dig for artifacts. We've got a mystery to solve and we don't have many days left to do it. Anyway, I'm not really interested in finding Allies, are you? I only said that stuff to throw Harriet off. We have to find out why someone or some *thing* doesn't want us in the Shaniko School."

"Yeah, well okay," Paige said, moistening her dry lips. "It definitely looks like somebody's hiding something, doesn't it?" Her t-shirt shivered in the hot wind.

Meggie had been thinking the same thing.

"Maybe they're hiding a ghost, Meggie."

Shaniko Hotel

CHAPTER 5

The Cellar

It was almost dinnertime and Aunt Abby still hadn't returned. Meggie and Paige decided to pack up some food and leave a note so she wouldn't worry. They were ready to return to the school. It was time to capture the Shaniko ghost.

The two detectives circled around behind the tall, steel-framed fire bell tower next to the City Hall to make last minute plans. Meggie passed the three barred cell doors of the old jail on the first floor and shivered, then glanced back toward the hotel, hoping Harriet hadn't seen them.

"Got everything?" she asked Paige who held her club in one hand and sack of food in the other.

"Yup." Paige was swinging her club like she was headed up to bat in a ball game at recess.

"Don't clobber me with that thing, Paige. You've got at least twenty nails sticking out of it."

Paige grinned. "We ran out of nails or I would've used more."

"If it's a ghost, that club won't do a thing."

"Oh great," Paige snorted, gazing down at her masterpiece. "I probably just wasted some perfectly good nails."

"I know."

In a few minutes they reached the school. "Well, here goes," Paige said, drawing a deep breath and hoisting Meggie up onto the roof.

Meggie pulled Paige up, then crawled in through the window. She could hardly believe she wasn't at least getting close to a dead faint. Maybe she and Paige were getting stronger. Smarter. Maybe that's what happened to ghost town detectives if they didn't just give up.

Sure. Maybe that was it. Maybe a little bit of the Wild West was creeping into her bloodstream. Paige's too. *This is almost exciting,* she said silently, leading the way through the dust and cobwebs of the abandoned school once again.

Suddenly everything changed. Paige almost fell over her best friend who had stopped dead in her tracks.

Meggie stared at the blackboard. She couldn't scream. She couldn't move.

One more chalk-white scrawl issued the final, ghostly warning:

DEATH TO THOSE WHO RETURN

She gasped and whirled around, nearly knocking Paige flat.

By now, Paige had seen it too. Dust flying, they scrambled out the window and down the roof like two frantic lizards, dropping their food—the club. Everything. But that wasn't important now. They were alive. *Alive!*

"Oh Meggie!" Paige said the minute they reached the back of the Pioneer Saloon. "What's goin' on?"

Meggie braced herself against an old door, her mind reeling, her heart pounding. Sweat crawled down her back like wet eels. *Death? No. I can't believe this.*

"We'd better tell Aunt Abby," Paige went on. "This isn't fun-and-games anymore."

Meggie nodded in complete agreement. She still couldn't speak. Couldn't think.

But Aunt Abby didn't return until dark and when she got back she just wanted to go to bed.

"We have to talk to you, Aunt Abby!" Meggie said. "Something *very* important."

"I'm just beat," she told the girls. "This eastern Oregon heat wipes me out. Can it wait until morning?"

"It's pretty important," Paige put in.

"Yeah," Meggie added, choosing her words carefully. "We made a discovery today."

"You did?" Her aunt's grey-green eyes brightened and she smiled. "Well, so did I. Old Shaniko coins, maybe twenty-five or thirty. They're called Allies. It's a nice find."

"I think we found something even more important than that, Aunt Abby."

"Yeah," Paige added. "We're almost positive there's a ghost here in Shaniko. We heard it howling in the school last night."

Aunt Abby blinked, wiping some damp, frizzy gray-blonde hair from her forehead. "A ghost?"

"Yes, and it's leaving messages," Meggie added. "On the chalk board in the old school." She knew they'd better level with her aunt. This wasn't junior detective material anymore.

"Oh, I see. Yes, messages on the blackboard. HAPPY NEW YEAR,

1937...KILROY WAS HERE, that sort of thing, mmmm? Well how did you girls get into the school? Certainly you didn't break in, did you?"

"Break in? Oh, we wouldn't even *think* of doing something like that, Aunt Abby," Paige said, catching Meggie's blank stare. "But there was this wide-open window without any glass right smack over a cellar roof..."

"Yeah, it wasn't boarded up or anything," Meggie added quickly. "And the roof was perfect. You know, like this little ladder just waiting to be climbed."

Aunt Abby smiled and got up from the picnic table. "Well, that's good," she said, heading for the van. "Because you know the rules—you know you can't disturb anything without permission. Even a consulting archaeologist like myself has to get permission and permits whenever I'm looking for artifacts. Goodnight girls," she said with a yawn, her crinkly eyes smiling. "Have a good sleep."

As soon as she had shut the door behind her, Meggie faced Paige. "She didn't even hear us. She didn't get it."

"I think she's too tired. We can tell her after she has her coffee in the morning. She's usually more normal then."

"Kilroy was here. Gee." Meggie rolled her eyes, splashing her face clean in the wash basin. "Who's Kilroy anyway?"

"I think it was somebody who used to go around leaving messages in the olden days when Aunt Abby was young."

Meggie brushed her teeth, then grabbed her book and crawled into the tent. She read awhile, then turned out the light and stared at the moon shafts sliding through the window. Darkness fell quickly but the bright moon lit up the valley like a street lamp. Maybe they should be in the van with the doors locked tonight. Was it even safe here in the tent?

Suddenly, Meggie heard it again. "Paige?" she whispered. "Did you hear that?"

Paige didn't answer.

"Paige, *the ghost!*" Meggie grabbed her sheet. "I think it's that ghost howling again!"

"Yeah. Right. Fine." Paige sat up. "So I hear it, too. So now what?" Her dark eyes were as round as two buckwheat pancakes.

"Okay, so let's go. Tonight. Let's sneak over to the school and maybe we'll find out where it's coming from at least." Meggie couldn't believe she was saying this. Feeling this way. Again.

Paige hesitated, then spoke. "I wonder if it's coming from the bell tower?"

"I don't know." Meggie reached for her cutoffs at the foot of her sleeping bag, slipping them on under her oversized t-shirt which also doubled as a nightshirt.

Slipping into their sneakers, they grabbed their flashlights and crept out into the moonlight. Meggie gazed around and felt a shiver.

Straggly locust trees whispered like evil specters in the wind and the yellow sage had a faint, foreboding glow. But it didn't matter. They had to know. They just had to. Meggie drew a deep breath, locking arms with Paige. Quietly, sure-footedly they moved up the deserted street, past the antique car museum and wagon yard on the right, the shops and hotel on the left. Meggie paused and adjusted her glasses, staring at the silhouette of the school in the shadows beyond. Her heart pounded.

She turned to Paige whose eyes were still huge. But Paige nodded. She was still one-hundred percent with Meggie. They both knew what they had to do. Keeping low, they crossed the road and crept closer to the old school with its odd, flat-topped roof and witch-hat tower. A lone flagpole extended upward toward the night sky. Meggie paused against the gatepost and glanced at the skull-like water tower hovering to their left in the shadows beyond. The wooden building looked like a huge casket sitting on a pedestal. It felt to her as though the square, black window-eyes watched them. She felt a chill and turned away, forcing the gruesome thoughts aside. Sneaking back into that school at midnight was crazy, but they had to do it. They had to know.

"You look like a ghost in that baggy nightshirt," Paige whispered. "All we need is one more ghost."

"Whaaa?" Meggie almost choked.

"I said, you look like a..."

"Be *quiet*, Paige." The pale flag shivered in the wind. Was it warning them? *Should we just go back and forget the whole thing?*

Suddenly a ghostly howl split the silence. She grabbed Paige's arm and squeezed tight.

"That is *not* Kilroy," Paige whispered, steadying herself against her best friend. "Noooo, that is definitely not Kilroy."

"But it's coming from the tower, isn't it?" Meggie added, trying to hear her feeble words over the pounding of her heart. "Okay—okay, so why don't you check it out? I'll, uh—I'll stay here and stand guard."

"What?" Paige whirled around and faced her best friend. "No way. You check it out and I'll stand guard." Dark, short hair quivered and framed the wide eyes.

"Paige Morefield, are you scared?"

"I think so."

"Yeah?" Meggie licked her dry lips. Well she was too. In fact she was so scared she could hardly breathe. "We shouldn't have come," she said finally, wondering if Paige could hear her teeth rattling.

"Okay then, let's check it out in the morning," Paige whispered, her eyes as round as the big yellow moon that kept slipping in and out of the clouds. "I..."

But before Paige could finish, a ghoulish creaking slithered up from the ground like a snake.

The cellar door opened slowly.

Water Tower

CHAPTER 6

The Shadow Speaks

Meggie fell backwards, knocking Paige flat onto the ground. Scrambling and clawing like two frantic muskrats caught in a trap, they struggled to get up. Then a voice spoke from the shadows.

"I told you to get out!"

Meggie froze, listening to the eerie words slither up from the darkness and strike out like nasty little vipers. Her fingers gripped the dirt and rocks until her knuckles hurt.

"OUT!"

"Yoweeee!" Paige gasped, leaping up. Dust and rocks flying, she took off running, but Meggie beat her back to the campsite.

"That su-sure didn't sound li—like a ghost to me!" Paige cried, skidding around the corner of the outhouse.

Meggie couldn't speak. Should they wake her aunt?

"It—uh, it sounded like Bluebeard, Meggie!"

"Huh?" Meggie whirled around and stared at her best friend.

"Bluebeard," Paige whispered hoarsely. "Haven't you ever read that story? He locks his wives in the tower. They always hear him coming up the steps. Thump...thump...thump..."

"Stop that, Paige!"

"Okay, then, if you know so much, who was it?"

Meggie drew a deep breath, trying to keep her voice low. "I'm not sure. But, you're right, that wasn't a ghost. What we saw *wasn't* a ghost."

"Yeah, okay. And maybe it wasn't Bluebeard, either. He'd be in the tower instead of the cellar, anyhow. Hey, wait a minute. I think that howling did come from the tower."

"Paige, be quiet." Meggie tried to think straight and Bluebeard wasn't helping. The warm Shaniko wind turned her sweat cold as they stood together underneath the moon. *Yes, the howling was coming from the tower, wasn't it? So who was in the cellar?*

"We have to go back. We have to find out," Meggie said matter-of-factly.

"*Now?*"

"Yeah, Paige."

"Oh, gross. Are you are serious, Meggie?"

Meggie braced herself, then turned and started back toward the school. Her knees felt like jelly, but they had to know. "If we don't find out tonight, maybe we'll never get another chance." Maybe it wasn't safe, but if that was so, then it probably wasn't safe in the tent, either.

Sure-footedly, they retraced their steps, moving cautiously toward the school. Meggie watched for movement. The tower. A window. The cellar door.

Then Paige grabbed her nightshirt. Meggie whirled around and watched the tall figure emerge from the cellar.

"I told you to leave!" the voice snarled from the shadows.

Terrified, Meggie backed up slowly, Paige still clinging to her shirt. This definitely was not a ghost.

"Get out!" he said again.

"That's *not* Bluebeard," Paige whispered.

"*Be quiet, Paige*," she said through tight lips, her pulse pounding so loud she could scarcely hear herself think.

"Uh—why? Yes, uh—so, why do you want us to get out?" Meggie tried to keep from choking on her words.

The form stepped out from the shadows, jet black eyes catching the moon's reflection. Meggie gasped, staring at the husky frame of a guy who couldn't have been more than thirteen or fourteen years old. *A kid. It's only a guy!*

"I said get out. Go!" The strong chin held firm.

"Hey, wait a minute!" It was Paige now. "You're not in charge of this school. Or us."

The eyes stared hard into Paige's face, but Meggie caught the flicker of fear. The slight quiver of the chin.

"Nobody's supposed to be in this school," Paige went on, growing bolder by the second. "Including you. Now, if you don't explain what's going on, I'm going to call the Burntoven County Sheriff. Or maybe the Swat Team at Hay Creek Valley."

"No."

Meggie's chin dropped. *Wait a minute—is he scared?* It was so dark she could scarcely tell, but it was as though this guy with jet-black hair and eyes had suddenly turned as pale as a ghost. *A ghost. Wait a minute. Is this the ghost? Is this overgrown nerd the "ghost of Shaniko?"*

"Get real," he said to Paige, "there isn't any Swat Team at Hay Creek Valley. There's no such place."

"She meant Grass Valley," Meggie cut in. "Now, you'd better tell us what's going on or there's gonna be trouble."

"Right," Paige said. "Major serious big-time trouble."

Turning abruptly, he started down into the cellar. "Follow me," he said. "I'll tell you but you can't tell anybody."

"Fair enough," Paige replied, following him down into the darkness.

"Wait a minute, Paige!" Meggie drew back. What were they getting themselves into, anyway? *We shouldn't be doing this. We could be walking right into a trap.*

"Paige!" Meggie stumbled behind her best friend, trying to grab her shirt, trying to stop her. "Paige, we shouldn't..."

"No, Meggie. We have to know," she said firmly, brushing Meggie's arm aside.

The wind slammed the cellar door shut behind them. Meggie's flesh crawled.

He led the way into the shadows beneath the school, gripping his flashlight in one hand and Paige's club in the other.

"Hey, wait a minute! Paige blurted. "That's my club!"

"Yeah, sure. Here." He turned and handed it to her like he was giving her a bouquet of sagebrush. "You dropped it."

Yes. They had dropped it, hadn't they? Dropped it when they ran out of the school. So this nerdy guy is the person who wrote those messages on the chalkboard—those warnings. She ducked under some cobwebs and winced. *What are we doing down here anyhow? This still might be a trap.*

"Okay, so what's goin' on?" Paige asked. Her dark eyes flashed in the shadows.

"If I tell you, you have to promise you won't tell a living soul. If you do, he'll come for you too."

Meggie cringed. "He?"

"Okay," Paige told him. "I promise."

No. Wait a minute, Paige. Don't promise anything. Meggie groped for Paige's arm but her best friend wasn't having any of it.

"Who's coming?" Paige asked. "Who's HE?"

Dark, hooded eyes narrowed and held her gaze. "The whipman."

"The Whoa...Whip...Whaaaa...?" Meggie's words spilled out like broken glass on the earth floor.

"Shhh!" he ordered, motioning her quiet. "The whipman. He hears. He knows..."

Meggie swallowed her fear and listened.

"He's coming for me."

CHAPTER 7

The Whipman

"We'll call 911 on our aunt's cell phone!" Paige exploded. "It'll probably take awhile for them to get here, but you can hide in our van, and if he breaks down the door, then I've got this club!" She held it up in the darkness like a beacon in the storm. "Or we can drive to…"

"No!" His fists tightened, his black eyes flashed. "No! They can't help. The whipman has complete power over everyone. Everything. He's heard the stick by now. He's coming!"

"Heard the whaaat?" Meggie stepped back.

"Wait a minute. Wait a minute!" Paige waved her hands. "The stick? What stick? I think you just lost me with the part about the stick."

Yeah. He just lost me, too. Has this guy got potato chips for brains or something?

"Somebody put the stick over my door. Sometimes that happens on the reservation when a person does something really bad. The spirit of the stick calls the whipman. He comes with his whip. He beats the kid and he does it in front of everybody."

"Oh my gosh, that's gross!" Paige burst out. "Did you do something

44

really bad?" Her eyes were growing wider by the second.

He nodded.

"Hey, wait a minute," Meggie put in. "This doesn't make any sense. Sticks don't talk. You're talking like you've been reading too many Gargoyle comic books."

He turned to Meggie, his dark eyes boring down on hers. "Bushtn!" he snorted. "It doesn't make any sense to you because you're not Native American. You don't know the ways of my people."

Bushtn? Native American? Meggie drew back and swallowed the unfamiliar words stuck in her throat. *Bushtn? Ways of my people? What's he saying? What does he mean?*

"The whipman is for real," he went on, his eyes still dark, piercing. "The whipman lives near the Warm Springs reservation, and even though he doesn't come much anymore, he's real. He comes if he's called."

"Native American? Are you Native American?" Paige asked, her brown eyes growing wider by the second. It was almost too dark to see much of anything, but Meggie knew Paige felt as confused as she did.

He nodded, knotting his soiled tank top with a firm hand. Strong legs stood their ground beneath his ragged cutoffs.

"Wow. Does the stick really and truly call him?" Paige was shaking her head back and forth, clearly impressed.

He nodded.

"I—I can't believe that," Meggie put in. "Something else is going on. A stick just doesn't do that."

"Who put the stick up there?" Paige went on, brushing Meggie's words aside like cobwebs.

"I'm almost positive it was my stepmother," he replied, his chin firm, his body rigid. "She's evil."

"Stepmother?" Paige was in his face now.

He nodded and backed away. "My dad just married her and it's like she's cast this spell on him. He's turned totally stupid. He's like a zombie with this twenty-four-hour smile on his face. He never hears anything I say anymore. He's totally out of it."

"A wicked stepmother?" Paige persisted. "Sort of like in Hansel and Gretel, maybe?"

"*Hansel and Gretel*?" Meggie turned to Paige and frowned.

"Yeah, the wicked stepmother convinces their father to take Hansel and Gretel into the woods and leave them there to die," Paige reminded her. "And they didn't even do anything bad."

"Paige, we're getting off the subject. This is confusing enough without throwing in Hansel and Gretel."

"No," Paige shot back. "No, we're not getting off the subject, Meggie."

"Get real, Paige. Hansel and Gretel is a Fairy Tale."

"Well, this isn't," he interrupted, wiping a nervous sweat off his face with the back of his hand. "This is for real. And she's probably a lot like that bad stepmother in your story, too. She's really cruel. I know she put that stick over my door. She wants him to come and whip me. To make a fool out of me in front of everyone." He bit his lip and turned away. "And, there's more. I had to leave."

Meggie wanted to understand. She wanted to believe him, but this was totally off the wall. And yet he seemed so sincere. Even scared. "So what did you do that was so bad?" she asked finally.

"I can't tell you."

Meggie fell silent.

Paige fidgeted, then spoke. "You're not a murderer or anything, are you? We're not supposed to talk to strangers, especially if they're murderers."

"Paige."

He shook his head and dropped his gaze. "I stole something. But it was mine once."

"That's not bad. I mean, that's not *real* bad, is it?" Paige told him.

"It was stealing." His eyes flashed above the high cheekbones in the pale light and he turned away. "I don't want to talk about it. I just need some more food before I split. Uh, by the way, thanks for the breakfast cereal and stuff you've been droppin' around. It sure beats the Dumpster behind the hotel."

"The Dumpster?" It was Meggie now. She realized that if he was eating garbage then he really had to be desperate. "Sure, we'll get..."

But before she could finish speaking, a blood-curdling howl shattered the darkness. *Oh no—not again.*

"The ghost!" Paige exploded, groping backward toward the cellar door.

"Yeah," he said thickly, tossing back his dark hair and staring upward into the shadows. "I have to get outta here but I need some food! Can you get me some?"

"Sure," Meggie said, backing up. "Ten minutes. We'll meet you behind the Pioneer Saloon in ten minutes!" *Anything to get out of this freaky place. Anything.*

"Okay, but hurry!" he called, disappearing into the shadows. "Hurry!"

CHAPTER 8

Nightstalker

Meggie and Paige got back to the campsite and scrounged around, throwing as much food into the sack as they could without waking up their aunt. Meggie glanced at her watch and slid the cooler back into the storage trailer. It must be close to midnight.

"We could tell her it was for Kilroy," Paige whispered, stuffing a half loaf of bread on top of the fruit and lunchmeat.

Meggie frowned, knowing that wasn't going to work.

"Or, we could just say we met Kilroy and he was really hungry. Then we could explain that Kilroy wasn't his real name." Paige paused, looking confused. "Hey, wait a minute, Meggie. We don't even know his name."

"I know," she replied, adding a bag of tortilla chips. *We're meeting this stranger at midnight behind a saloon. It's crazy. Lame. Nuts.*

They started back, each carrying a sack of food.

"And, can you believe he's been in there with that ghost the whole time?" Paige went on, her shirt shivering in the breeze. "Plus the whapman following him."

"Whipman."

"Yeah, well whip or whap—two at once would freak me out," she said as she leaped over some sagebrush. "No wonder he's gotta get out of Shaniko."

"Over here," the voice said from the shadows. He stepped out from behind a shed.

Meggie almost fell over Paige. *This guy can slide out of the darkness like a...a...* She forced her grim thoughts aside and handed him the sacks of food.

"Thanks," he said, grabbing them quickly. But Meggie could tell he was thankful, knowing the stale bread was probably a whole lot better than the garbage he'd been getting out of the Dumpster.

"We don't even know your name," Paige said, moving closer.

"Gabe," he told them, "but don't breathe a word because..." He stopped and motioned them quiet.

Meggie felt the tension split the air. "What?"

"Shhh!" he said sharply, motioning them down behind an oil drum.

Meggie and Paige hit the ground like rocks.

"What's wrong?" Paige whispered.

"Look!" he said thickly, pointing to the school grounds in the distance. A man's shadow moved quietly, skulking through the grass. Long, stringy hair flew like a mane from beneath a wide-brimmed hat.

Meggie threw her hand over her mouth, stifling a gasp.

"It's *him*," he said, moving further back into the shadows. His voice quivered like the bunchgrass in the wind.

"H—Him?" Paige almost choked on the word. But Meggie knew. They both knew he meant the whipman.

"He's here. *He found me.*" Gabe got up slowly, backing into the shadows.

"But—wait a minute, are you *sure?*" Meggie struggled. "I mean, it's too far for us to know for absolute positive sure, don't you think?"

He shook his head grimly, dark straight hair catching the moon's reflection. "I can tell."

"Maybe it's some guy who needs a place to sleep," Paige put in.

"At midnight in the middle of the desert? No, it's him. It's the whipman and he's come for me."

"Then you have to hide!" It was Meggie now.

He reeled around and faced her. "Sure!" he laughed ruefully. "Any ideas?"

Meggie's mind raced. *No. Not the tent. The tent would probably be the first place somebody like that would think of. He'd be easy prey in the tent. Besides, we'd need to get permission from Aunt Abby before we try to hide somebody in our tent. Not the van either. She needs her sleep and besides, she'd never believe all this anyway. Okay—so that won't work. Then, what about the saloon?* Meggie gazed around in the shadows, her mind still racing. *No. He needs to get away from here. He's not safe.*

"What about the wool barn?" Paige put in.

"The wool barn?" Meggie turned and gazed at the silhouette of the huge, empty warehouse looming behind them in the distance. She remembered Aunt Abby telling them how the early settlers brought and stored their wool and wheat there. "It's pretty big. Yeah, maybe he could hide out in there. Aunt Abby said it was supposed to be the biggest wool warehouse in the whole state of Oregon."

"It's really huge," Paige went on. "Nobody'd find you—at least not until morning. Hey, wait a minute. It's locked up."

Paige was right. They had checked out the wool barn when they first came to Shaniko.

"Locks aren't gonna keep me out." Dark straight hair fell across his clouded eyes. "If it's empty, I'll get in. And, uh—well thanks. Thanks a lot for everything." He backed into the shadows. "And don't forget your promise," he said to Paige.

"Promise?"

"To keep our secret. You can't tell anybody."

Meggie drew back, then turned to Paige. "Oops, well, see—we can't keep secrets like that," she explained. "I mean, we have to tell our aunt at least."

"No. You can't!" His hooded eyes darkened. "Besides, if you tell, he'll come for you, too."

For us? Meggie froze, her shirt quivering in the wind.

And then he disappeared, swallowed up by the shadows lying under the moon.

Meggie whirled around and faced her best friend. "Paige Morefield, how come you promised him that? You know we have to tell Aunt Abby when important things like this happen. Now what're we gonna do?"

"Shhh!" Paige yanked her shirt, pulling her down. "Look!" Paige pointed toward the school in the distance.

Meggie swallowed her words, then turned and gazed toward the shadows beyond. The man had disappeared. "Where'd he go?" she whispered hoarsely.

"I don't know," Paige whispered back. "But let's not hang around and find out!"

They crouched low, weaving behind the buildings and through the wagon yard like two frantic sage hens in nightshirts. "If that whipguy knows where we are, we're zip," Paige said, diving into the tent and landing on Meggie.

"Take it easy, Paige! Meggie said, taking off her glasses and pushing Paige over on to her own sleeping bag. "How do I know what whipmen do? I've never seen one before. I've never even heard of such a thing. This is beyond weird, Paige."

"I know. The whipman is even worse than Bluebeard."

"Paige, forget Bluebeard. Bluebeard is not the problem."

"I know. He goes for wives. It looks like the whipman goes for kids. Like us."

"Paige. Bluebeard isn't real and the whipman *is*. He's creeping around out there looking for that poor kid."

"And *us* if we tell. Oh Meggie, what're we gonna do?"

Meggie drew a deep breath and gazed hard into her best friend's face.

I wish I knew.

City Hall, Fire Bell Tower

CHAPTER 9

Bushtns

Meggie hardly slept. It was almost morning when she and Paige finally went to sleep. When they woke up, Aunt Abby had left on another dig. *Well, that takes care of having to tell her what happened last night,* Meggie realized, sitting up and glancing at her watch. *At least for now.* It was almost ten.

"Are you alive?" Paige muttered.

"Yeah."

"I think our problem is solved, Meggie. We can't tell Aunt Abby about the stuff that's been going on because she's already gone," Paige told her. "I heard the van leave." Meggie heard the gratitude in Paige's voice.

"But sooner or later we're going to have to tell her."

"Just hear me out," Paige went on. "He's probably gone by now anyway, and once he's gone it won't matter if we tell."

"Except you promised him you wouldn't." Meggie crawled out of her sleeping bag and gazed out the window of the tent toward the wool barn in the distance. "I just hope the whipman didn't find him."

"Yeah, me too. You think we should go check, Meggie?"

"In broad daylight? And have him follow us?"

"You mean Gabe?"

"No, the whipman, Paige."

Paige shrugged and got up. She grabbed a towel and crawled out into the bright morning.

Meggie's mind raced, wondering if he had escaped. Yet, if he did get away without being seen, then the whipman might still be snooping around Shaniko looking for him. The thought gave her the creeps.

After they had both cleaned up and eaten, they sat down to make plans.

"We can't do anything stupid just in case that stick *is* talking to him," Paige said, brushing her hair.

"Paige, I'm having trouble with that."

Paige pushed her words aside. "And how about Bushtns? What are *they*? Did you hear him say Bushtn, Meggie? Do you think it has something to do with the stick? Stick. Bush. They go together."

Meggie felt an odd chill. She hadn't even thought about that.

"Maybe the Stick follows the Bush—the Bushtn," Paige went on, her eyes growing wider and wider. "This is really beginning to freak me out, Meggie."

"Yeah, me too." Meggie got up and rummaged through the storage trailer, wondering if they'd brought a dictionary. But they hadn't.

"Bushtn might be something important," Paige put in. "Let's ask somebody who knows."

But most of the people walking around Shaniko were tourists and didn't know too many Native American words.

"The only Indian word I know is Wasco," a nice old man said as he twirled his white beard thoughtfully. "Means 'basin,' and don't ask me why. Shaniko is in Wasco County."

"Thanks," Paige said, nodding.

"Okay, Basin is not Bushtn," Meggie said finally. She knew they shouldn't be stirring up any suspicion by asking the locals, but they weren't getting anywhere with the tourists.

"I'll bet Harriet knows," Paige said. "She knows everything around here."

"I know. Maybe too much." Meggie glanced over at the café where she waited tables. "I'm not sure about her, Paige. Especially after our little incident yesterday."

"We could act like it was nothing," Paige put in. "Be real cool, y'know? I'll do it, Meggie. We need to know. Bushtn might be a clue. It could even save our lives."

Meggie agreed, wishing they could come up with a better idea than asking Harriet. But they couldn't, so they walked over to the café and ordered some lemonade.

Harriet filled their glasses and took their money. She wasn't smiling. "Anything else?" she asked, straightening her stiff, unbending hair.

"Uh, oh yeah. We forgot. How about a Bushtn?" Paige asked. "Yes, two Bushtns with french fries and catsup, please."

"Whaaat?" Harriet drew back, nearly dropping the pitcher of lemonade.

"Uh, skip the catsup," Paige added quickly.

Meggie almost choked. "*Paige, you are not doing this right,*" she said between clenched teeth.

"You can leave," Harriet said coldly. "Now."

Meggie tried to apologize, but the words got stuck in her throat.

But apologize for what? What had they done?

"It's something bad," Paige said the minute they were out on the porch. Even the old windows framed against the brick wall of the hotel seemed to be arched in dismay.

As they started across the street, Meggie glanced over her shoulder. Harriet stood in the doorway, eyes narrowed, chin set—glaring like a bull antelope ready to charge.

"She knows we know," Paige said out of the corner of her mouth.

"Know *what*?"

"That's the problem. We don't know. Except she really freaked when we said that word."

Meggie bit her lip and glanced back one last time. Harriet still stood there, her dark eyes boring down on them. "Paige, we have to do something. Whipman or not, we have to find Aunt Abby. She'll help us. She'll know what Bushtn means."

But they couldn't find her or the van anywhere. Meggie figured she must be digging at a site near Burntoven or Cross Hollows. Or maybe she went to Antelope to get supplies.

"If Aunt Abby doesn't get back before dark, then let's go to the wool barn," Paige said as they neared the campground. "We can wait until dark. That way nobody will follow us. If Gabe's not there, then we'll know he got away."

"The wool barn? Tonight?"

Paige nodded.

Meggie wasn't sure this was such a great idea, especially if that creepy whipman still happened to be hanging around in the shadows somewhere. And what about the Bushtn? Would *he* be hiding in the wool barn too? Meggie felt an odd chill, glancing sideways toward the old structure looming like a huge wooden coffin in the distance. And who—or *what* was the Bushtn, anyway? Was there some connection between the Bushtn and the whipman? If it wasn't for Gabe, Meggie knew she wouldn't even be thinking about going back to that place tonight.

They asked a few more passersby if they knew what Bushtn meant, but only got blank looks, so they finally gave up and went back to the campsite to wait.

"He's Native American, Meggie."

"Who?"

"Gabe."

"Yeah, I know," Meggie said, drawing a deep breath and picking up a book she had left on the portable camp table.

"But he's not like those wild Indians we saw in the Shaniko parade. Not at all."

Meggie nodded in complete agreement.

"He even gave me back my club," Paige went on. "That shows me a lot. If he wanted, he could've creamed us right then and there in the cellar."

Meggie hadn't thought of that. She nodded again, and went back to her book.

Shortly after lunch, Aunt Abby returned.

Relieved, Meggie walked over to the van. "You're just the person we want to see!"

Her aunt took off her straw hat and shook some dust from her hair. "Mmmm?" she smiled, heading over to the cooler to get some food. "You girls having fun?"

"Yes and no," Paige said.

"Ah? Still finding messages over in that school?" She seemed to be in a hurry.

"It wasn't Kilroy, Aunt Abby," Meggie put in, hoping for a way to explain it right.

"No?" Her aunt looked up, then back down into the half-empty cooler. "Say, are you two cleaning me out, here?"

Meggie drew a deep breath, her mind shifting back to the problem of taking the food to Gabe. "Uh, well, not exactly. You see we took some food over to the school."

"Which reminds me," Aunt Abby muttered, taking out a soda. "You kids are lucky you got into that school. Next summer you won't find any open windows to crawl into. I hear the locals are fixing it up. Going to use it for a community hall or some such thing. They're even getting a bell for the tower." She scavenged around for some lunch.

"Oh no! That's terrible!" Paige put in, frowning. "How come people always want to ruin a perfectly good ghost town by fixing it up?"

Aunt Abby shrugged, placed some food in a canvas bag and walked toward the van. "I suppose they just want to live here and enjoy it, don't you?" she said, plopping her straw hat back on her head. "After all, it's not a dead ghost."

"*Dead* ghost?" Meggie almost choked on the words.

Aunt Abby laughed. "Yes. A dead ghost is the term for a ghost town that's completely vacated. Dead. And Shaniko isn't. There are still a few people living here. Not many, but enough to run the hotel and café— a few shops and the Post Office. By the way, don't worry if I'm a bit late getting back. I'm meeting a few friends near Bend. Batty archaeologists just like myself. We just might get carried away telling lies, so don't wait up."

She climbed into the van and waved, driving off.

"They're gonna ruin Shaniko, Meggie—dead or alive, they're gonna ruin this town."

"Paige."

"Yeah?"

"Paige, we didn't find out about a Bushtn."

Paige threw up her arms. "Oh no—it's too late. She's gone!"

"I know."

"Then I guess we definitely have to go to the wool barn tonight. We have to find out."

Tonight? Paige's words hit Meggie smack in the face. She had almost forgotten. "You think we should? You *really* think we should, Paige?"

"Yeah."

Meggie drew a deep breath and let the words settle in. The wool barn. Tonight. She watched her friend open the cooler and pull out some hard-boiled eggs, then crack and roll them as though she had just got back from an Easter egg hunt. *Paige is the brave one, isn't she? Fearless. Strong. And she's right. If we don't go tonight, we'll never know if Gabe needs help. Or if he got away.* Meggie tried not to think about the whipman. Or the Bushtn. She knew she had to be strong. Yes, Paige was right. They had to go.

For Gabe's sake, they had to. Tonight.

CHAPTER 10

Wild and Woolly Caper

As soon as it was dark they crept out into the quiet shiver of wind. Meggie's t-shirt trembled against the cold sweat of her excitement, her fear. She gazed on the barren horizon, dotted with shacks and sagebrush and the huge wool barn beyond.

"Let's go," Paige whispered, cutting across the road and circling behind the caboose.

Meggie followed, keeping alert. Shadows slithered across the bunchgrass and yellow sage as they moved behind some old buildings, including the antique car museum. She held her flashlight tight in one hand, knowing they might need it once they reached the wool warehouse. Moon shadows crept in and out from behind the clouds.

Meggie and Paige crossed the fields, keeping low. "It's humungous, isn't it?" Paige whispered as they neared the gray, wooden ghost of Shaniko's past.

Meggie nodded, her knuckles whitening. She gripped her flashlight tighter in her hand. Clouds scudded overhead as they neared the old structure where huge white letters on the roof spelled out the name

SHANIKO. Meggie gazed around, trying to shut out the moaning, creaking sounds growing louder and louder.

"What a creepy place," Paige whispered, crawling under the wire fence.

Meggie agreed, casting a quick backward glance to make sure they weren't being followed.

Suddenly a shadow moved. Her blood ran cold. Terrified, Meggie groped her way beneath the fence and grabbed Paige's arm, pointing at the dark form crouching like a cougar in the grass. Fear circled her throat. She couldn't speak. She couldn't move.

"It's me," the voice said from the shadows.

Meggie almost fainted with relief. It was Gabe. He was safe!

"I almost had a heart attack!" Paige sputtered. "You scared me to death!"

"Sorry."

"So—so you're still here, huh?" Meggie said as soon as she could get the words out of her throat.

He nodded in the shadows. "Yeah, it's a pretty cool place to hide."

"But, he's gonna find you," Paige put in. "Sooner or later the whipman's gonna find you."

"You got any better ideas?" he said flatly, his high cheekbones moist with sweat.

Meggie could tell he was scared, and who could blame him? "We'll help," she said finally, the silence stretching like black pitch between them.

But then Meggie saw his hesitation. "What's wrong?" she asked.

"I can't let you help me. There's something you don't know. Something you can't understand."

What was it? Meggie wondered, trying to block out the eerie moaning of the old barn in the wind. What else was Gabe hiding?

"But we want to help you," Paige put in, moving closer to the kid standing rigid against the shadows. "If you'll just let us."

He stood unmoving. Unspeaking.

"We want to be your friends," Meggie added. And she meant it.

Paige nodded in complete agreement. "Yeah, even if you do believe in sticks that talk and stuff like that. But how can we help you if we don't even know your name?"

"Stackpole. Gabe Stackpole."

"Well, I'm Meggie Bryson and this is my best friend Paige Morefield, and even though we might look like two ordinary sixth-graders, we're not. We're actually ghost town detectives. We can smell a mystery from ten miles away. And solve it faster than it takes to drop into a mine shaft."

"Or a sheep pen," Paige added.

Meggie turned to her friend. "Paige..."

"I'm listening," Gabe said.

"We *are* going to help you," Meggie went on. "But first you need to help us. You have to tell us what's going on."

"I can't."

"Why?"

"You'd never understand."

"I'd understand," Paige told him. "I believed you when you told me about your evil stepmother and the stick that talks. I'd believe anything. I even believe in Blue..."

But before she had finished her sentence, a nightmarish howl broke into her words, sending chills straight down to the bottom of Meggie's sneakers.

"Eeeyow!" Paige yelled, grabbing Meggie. "It's the ghost!"

"Follow us!" Meggie yelled, motioning to Gabe to follow them back to Shaniko. She felt the sting of the wind in her face, the burning, slithering shadows circling her throat as they crawled back under the fence and raced through the blackened fields toward the campground.

"If our aunt isn't back, you—you can hide in the tent!" Meggie called back to Gabe. She had taken the lead. Her feet flew. Her heart raced.

The broken down shacks and fences whipped by like phantoms in the wind. But when she and Paige reached the campsite, she discovered Gabe wasn't with them. "Whaaa?" Her eyes darted around, but he wasn't there. "Gabe?"

"Where is he, Paige? Where's Gabe?"

"I don't know! Oh, Meggie—I don't know!"

CHAPTER 11

The Secret Passage

What are we gonna do? Why isn't Aunt Abby back? Meggie's head reeled. Her heart raced. *And why hadn't Gabe followed them? Why?*

Paige and Meggie shivered in the tent. "You don't think he went back into that warehouse, do you?"

"And run smack into the ghost? Are you kidding?"

"But, why didn't he follow us?"

Meggie wished she knew. "Maybe he did. Maybe he started to follow us and then..."

"And then what?"

"Oh, Paige!"

"What?" Paige moved closer. "What is it, Meggie?"

Meggie paled, knowing she had to say it. She had to. "Maybe *he's* got Gabe."

"He?"

Meggie's throat tightened. Paige already knew, didn't she? They both knew.

Paige bit her lip and turned away. "You mean—the whipman."

"We have to do something," Meggie went on, peering through the screened window of the tent into the darkness. "Paige, we can't just leave him out there!"

"I know. I know! We'll go back. Yes. I'll take my club and we'll go back!" Paige retrieved her handmade weapon at the foot of her sleeping bag.

Meggie took some deep breaths, trying to calm herself. Who'd ever think this ghost town was turning out to be so dangerous? Nice quiet little Shaniko, Oregon. Nice quiet little wool capital gone to sleep. She was beginning to wonder if maybe Paige wasn't so far off track with her funky Bluebeard story after all. Bluebeard? Bushtns? And what else? The fairy-tale might be turning into a nightmare.

"We can also use our flashlights for weapons!" Paige said, waving her spiked club in one hand and her flashlight in the other.

Meggie's thoughts shifted. She turned to her best friend. "Paige, I don't think that club is gonna do it."

Paige looked down at her club with nail heads sticking out in every direction. "I think it's pretty cool."

"Probably not for a whipman, though."

"Why not? Since when did you become an expert on weapons for whipmen? Besides, maybe it's the ghost that's got Gabe, anyway."

Her words jarred Meggie. "Wait a minute, Paige—if it's the ghost, then the club is definitely going to be a joke."

"Well, I'm keeping the joke in one hand and my flashlight in the other. Now, are you ready, Megan Bryson?"

"Yeah. Right." Meggie picked up her flashlight and unzipped the tent. Paige always called her Megan when things got serious. And this happened to be one of those times, didn't it? She gripped her flashlight tight in her sweaty hand and led the way out into the darkness.

Once again, they set out into the shadows—into the warm, eerie wind that shivered the locust trees and sent the dry, prickly sagebrush crawling like insects across the bunchgrass. Clouds scudded overhead, sending moon shadows slithering over the ground. It was like Halloween in August.

Meggie stepped carefully over the rock scabs on the high grassy flat, moving quickly and quietly past the dark wooden bones of fallen, crumbling structures. The wind gave them voices—moaning, creaking voices that seemed to be calling out from the shadows. Her flesh crawled. She picked up her pace, forcing her mind and her feet toward the huge dark warehouse in the distance. *Gabe, where are you? Are you okay?* Her eyes stung, blinking back the dust and fear and shadows surrounding them.

Suddenly Meggie felt a sharp nudge. "Whaaa...?"

"Shh!" Paige whispered crouching behind a huge, ugly scab of rock and motioning frantically for Meggie to turn out her flashlight.

Meggie caught her breath and flicked it off, following Paige's trembling finger pointing to the shadows behind them. And then she saw it.

Oh no. It's him. The whipman!

She watched him slither out from behind the antique car museum. His black stringy hair caught the reflection of the moon, waving like dark, spider fingers from underneath the hat. Waving. Reaching. Coming...

Fear held her to the ground. *We have to run. We have to.*

Paige squeezed her arm. She understood.

Dirt, rocks and sagebrush flying, they raced toward the wool barn. Meggie prayed they'd find some way to get inside and hide, prayed

Gabe was there. "Gabe!" Meggie screamed. "Gabe! Gabe! He's coming! He's following us!"

She could scarcely hear the sounds of her screams, feel the sting of rocks and grass and sharp wire fence against her slender arms and legs. *Please let him be there! Please.*

"Gabe! Where are you?" Paige yelled. Short, dark hair whirled like little dust devils above her small, wiry frame as she leaped over rocks, racing like a wild, erratic gust of wind. "Gabe! Gabe!"

Then Meggie saw him. Skidding to a halt, she watched Gabe's shadow move out from the back corner of the wool barn. Arms waving, he gestured frantically for them to follow.

Meggie grabbed Paige's shirt and motioned her toward the back corner of the warehouse. "It—it's him, Paige! It's Gabe!" she cried out, her words throbbing with joy, her heart pounding with hope. Circling around to the backside of the huge rectangular structure, they found him crouching beside what appeared to be a cellar window, motioning for them to follow. Rusty old bins and machinery threw long, bizarre shadows from behind.

"Oh...Wow! You're still here!" Meggie and Paige cried, their words choking in the dust, tumbling together like a wild, happy avalanche.

"And you're okay!" Meggie exploded. "We're so glad you're okay!"

"Shhh Bushtn!" he said, ordering them quiet. His dark eyes narrowed as he gazed around. "Now follow me!" He motioned them into the narrow passage.

Bushtn? Meggie froze. She couldn't move. *He said it again. What is it? Is a Bushtn following them too? Is a Bushtn closing in on them just like the whipman?* Her head spun around, her pulse pounded.

"Follow me!" he said again, his dark gaze holding Meggie's.

"But—but the ghost!" Paige cried, drawing back.

"Shh!" he said again. "Don't worry! We're safe. For now, at least. Just follow me. It's a secret passage."

Dirt and webs and darkness encircled them as they crawled through the rough, dry tunnel beneath the old warehouse. Meggie crawled directly behind Gabe and Paige brought up the rear. Musty, stale smells of wool and hides and rotting wood assaulted her senses, while pale shadows from Gabe's flashlight slithered ahead like laughing, taunting ghosts. She felt as though she was being squeezed— smothered by some dark, ancient doom closing in.

And then she heard it again. Faint but clear. The eerie, wailing howl of the ghost crept down through the tunnel like the snake of death.

Were they trapped?

CHAPTER 12

The Trap Door

Meggie didn't move. *It's here. The ghost is here in the warehouse waiting for us.* Her sweat felt cold against the smothering fear, cold against the strangle of panic rising within her.

"Keep moving," Gabe said.

"No!" Meggie choked. "He—it—don't you hear it?"

"It's okay. We'll be safe. Just keep moving. Keep following me."

"Safe?" It was Paige now and she wasn't moving one inch. "That's a *ghost* howling up there, Gabe Stackpile!"

"Stack*pole.*"

"Yeah, okay. Stackpole—pile. It doesn't matter. What matters is you're asking us to face...*death.*"

"It's not what you think. It's not gonna hurt you!" he called back roughly. "It—he's my—my friend. Now keep following me!"

"Your *friend?*" Meggie choked.

"Shh!" he ordered, moving on.

I've heard it all, Meggie said, swallowing her words, and crawling on into the darkness. *I can't believe this. His friend! First the stick that talks, then a Bushtn and now a ghost who's his friend? No. It's crazy. Nuts.*

"Did you hear that, Meggie?" Paige whispered, moving closer. "Did you hear what he just said?"

Meggie nodded, still holding back the words and scrambled thoughts that were crawling around like worms in her head. Yes. She'd heard. She knew they were entrusting their lives into the hands of a Native American kid who could be leading them down a dark tunnel of death—where spirits, Bushtns, ghosts waited.

And yet, what choice do we have? Are we supposed to back up and face the whipman who's probably creeping around in the shadows just outside?

Meggie's flesh crawled as she moved on into the dark passage, still struggling with her fears, her confusion, the unknown.

In moments, they came to a trap door. Gabe crawled upward, motioning for them to follow. Meggie felt the splintery wood on her hands as she inched toward the opening over her head. The gruesome howling had stopped as suddenly as it had started, yet she wasn't sure she wanted to face whatever they were going to have to face next. Planks and boards creaked in the wind, greeting them with unearthly, raspy voices. She eased up into the shadowy room and drew a deep breath, gazing around with wide, terror-filled eyes. Paige stayed close on her heels.

"Turn out your flashlights," Gabe whispered. "I think we're safe here."

Safe? Meggie swallowed her fear, gazing around the shadowy room piled high with rotten gunnysacks and boxes. Moonlight slid through the cracks and knotholes with sharp, pointing fingers.

"I still have my club," Paige said weakly, holding up the funky nails protruding from her stick. It looked like a punk rocker's hair. She was trying to smile as she watched Gabe close and bolt the trap door.

Meggie would have smiled back—even laughed—if she didn't feel like crying. Would a bolt or walls keep out ghosts and Bushtns—*and the whipman*? This was like a nightmare in slow motion.

Gabe switched out his flashlight and crept over to a knothole, peering out. "We don't want him to see the light coming through the cracks," he said in the pitch-black darkness.

"Wh—who?" Meggie grimaced, wondering which horrible thing he meant.

"The guy following you. The whipman. I saw him, too. He watched you—followed you when you split and headed back to the campground." Gabe was still glued to the knothole.

Paige gulped so loud Meggie thought it was a burp.

"So that's why you didn't follow us back?" Meggie said.

He hesitated, then turned and faced her. "Yes."

"But, the ghost," Paige put in. "I mean, you just walked straight back here with that thing wailing and—and…"

"I told you I can handle the ghost. It's not the ghost that's out to get me."

Meggie cringed, listening to him talk about the ghost like it was Anne of Green Gables. This was getting worse by the second.

Paige went on, "You see anything out there?"

"No," he said, kneeling down and looking through another, larger hole in the wall.

"So what next?" Paige asked, still holding the funky club in her hand like it was going to do some good. "Do we just wait in here until we starve to death and turn into skeletons?"

Paige had a point, Meggie realized. They couldn't stay here. If that whipman was anything like Gabe said, he'd find them. The dry, musty walls felt like they were closing in. It was just a matter of time.

"Why'd you come back?" he asked them both.

"Because we were scared something might've happened to you," Meggie replied.

He was silent for a few moments, then spoke. "Thanks."

They both nodded.

"Well, okay," Meggie said finally, "so, uh—back to what's going on. You say you've figured out the ghost, but what about the whipman?"

"Yeah," Paige agreed with a gulp. "He's gonna keep looking until he finds us, right?"

"Until he finds *me*," Gabe said to them. "It's me he's looking for."

Meggie drew a deep breath. "Except then how come he was following us?"

"Because he knows you'll lead him straight to me. You were hollering my name so loud you probably shook all the bats in the rafters loose."

Paige gulped again. "Yeah, right. But if this guy is getting his messages from sticks and weird stuff like that, then a little hiding place like this isn't gonna keep him out."

Gabe didn't answer.

"Plus, my aunt is probably back by now and she's gonna have a frizzy if we're not there," Meggie said. "She might even call the sheriff."

He turned away quickly.

Meggie wished she knew what he was thinking right then. *Sometimes he seems so strong and other times, it's like he's as scared as I am.*

Maybe even worse. And yet, could she blame him? *I'd die if a whipman got me and started whipping me in front of my friends. I'd flat-out die.*

"Then maybe if we go back, we can throw him off your trail," she said finally, wishing her words would quit shaking like her knees.

"I don't think anything's gonna do that," he replied. "But it's better if you two don't get involved anymore than you already have. I'll be okay."

Meggie gazed into the shadows, wondering if he would be, wondering if they could just walk out and leave him to this—this monster? Could he get away in time? She watched him standing rigid against the shadows and she knew he was scared. But if anybody could get out of a tight spot, maybe Gabe could. *He can slip in and out of shadows almost like a...ghost.* Meggie almost choked on the word.

"So, you mean, we're just supposed to go back out there with him waiting for us?" It was Paige now and her eyes were as wide as two knotholes. "We're supposed to go back—crawl back out that tunnel with—with..."

"No," he said, motioning to them both. "We're gonna follow some rafters overhead and get you to the other end of the warehouse. You'll have a better chance of getting away from there."

"And you can come with us," Meggie said, following him up onto a stair-step pile of boards and boxes. "We'll tell my aunt what happened and she'll figure out something."

"Yeah, she's really smart," Paige told him. "She's hangs out in ghost towns all the time and she's not scared of anything. But, uh..."

"But, what?" he asked.

"Well, even though she loves ghost towns, she doesn't believe in ghosts, which means she might have trouble with the part about the talking stick. But we could..."

"Paige."

"Yeah, well she will, Meggie. The talking stick is *not* going to fly."

"That's one of the reasons I'm not going with you," he told them both, reaching up toward the rafters and hoisting himself up. "I'll get you out of here and make sure you get back okay, then I'm gonna split."

"Split?"

"I have to go. Nobody's going to understand. Nobody."

"Except us," Meggie said, following him up into the eaves, thinking about Gabe instead of the spiders and bats that were probably crawling around. "You know we'll understand. If you'll only tell us everything, maybe we can help." She brushed some webs out of her hair and cringed.

"Yeah," Paige added, following Meggie like a small, sure-footed lizard. Her t-shirt caught on a huge splinter and she jerked it loose. "We're your friends."

He hesitated, then shook his head in the shadows. "You can't help me anymore, but thanks a lot for trying."

Suddenly they heard a noise below. A distant slam. Creaking.

Meggie froze.

Gabe drew a quick breath and motioned them quiet.

The whipman? Had he entered the warehouse? Was he waiting somewhere in the shadows below?

Was it too late to escape?

CHAPTER 13

The Attic

A rat crawled across a beam directly over Meggie's head. She stifled a scream.

Gabe grabbed her arm, silencing her.

No one moved.

Bracing herself, Meggie watched the black creature skitter into the shadows. *At least it wasn't the ghost. The ghost would have been worse,* she said silently, trying to find some scrap of comfort. This place was beyond creepy.

Gabe released his grip on her arm and motioned for her and Paige to follow. Pale shafts of moonlight lit the rough, dark attic path above the warehouse.

She drew a deep breath and followed him on, trying to push the thoughts of the whipman and rats and bats and ghosts out of her head. Huge cracks in the ceiling beneath them revealed they were above a gigantic room. It looked as though somebody had turned this old warehouse into a dance hall or gym. Meggie noticed a stage at the far end and a piano over in the corner. *He's probably down there right this minute. Hiding. Waiting for us.*

Paige clutched her club, crawling quietly, carefully behind Meggie. Meggie turned and saw her eyes, wide and bright.

Oh, gross. This is even scarier than Nighthawk, isn't it? Worse than that mine shaft. But we're gonna be okay. We are, Paige.

Could Paige know her thoughts? And the whipman—could he read their minds this very minute? Did he know they were directly overhead? *Does he know, even without hearing?* Meggie remembered what Gabe had said. Maybe Gabe was right about the whipman— about the stick that speaks to him. *Maybe there is such a thing and maybe the stick is talking to the whipman this very second and telling him exactly where we are.* She shuddered, then braced herself and peered down once again. But she didn't see anything below. She didn't hear any more noises except the faint creaking of the wind in the eaves. Meggie swallowed her fear and crawled on.

Once they reached the far end of the warehouse, Gabe stopped and beckoned them over to a far corner where an opening fell into the darkness below. "Wait," he whispered. "I'll signal if the coast is clear."

Meggie and Paige watched him disappear below, then return with a rope. Giving them the all-clear signal, he tossed it up. Meggie hooked the rope around a huge plank and shimmied down behind Paige.

"I think somebody lived here once," he said, keeping his voice low. "It's like somebody turned this old place into an apartment with shops and a dance floor and stuff like that. Down the hall there's a main door that leads outside."

"Oh, good." Paige sighed with relief.

"It's locked, though."

Meggie caught her breath and gazed around in the shadows.

76

"Then, how—?"

"I'll take care of it," he said quietly, slipping away.

"Maybe the Bushtn helps him with the locks," Paige suggested.

"Paige, I was trying to forget about the Bushtn. Why'd you have to bring him up? It's enough with the whipman and the ghost and the rats."

"At least I haven't brought up Bluebeard. You should be thankful for that, Meggie."

"Bluebeard!"

"Shhh, Meggie! The whipman's gonna hear us!"

Meggie swallowed her rush of words and whirled around. Gabe had returned.

"Hey, keep your voices down, okay? Now follow me."

Gabe led the way down some steps to the main door, opening it carefully and gazing around.

So locks don't keep Gabe Stackpole out. Or in.

They slipped out on to the old porch, keeping close to the wall. Meggie blinked, adjusting her eyes to the bright moon. Bunchgrass shivered on the dark moonlit horizon.

"I don't think I want to go back the way we came," Paige whispered, her eyes huge.

Meggie agreed. The ghostly shacks and buildings lurked in the shadows beyond—daring them to return along the same rock-scabbed path. Besides, he might still be back there. Waiting.

"Yeah, well I was thinkin' the same thing," Gabe told them, his eyes darting around like a hawk at midnight. "I figure your best move is to circle Shaniko and come in from the back side." He pointed to the outer perimeter of the town lying in the shadows.

"Okay," Meggie said, wishing there was another way. But there wasn't. She gazed at the dark, unknown path beyond and felt a chill.

"It's gonna take you longer, but you should be okay," he went on, interrupting Meggie's bleak thoughts. "Take care," he said to them both. "And uh—thanks for everything. Thanks a lot." And then he was gone.

"Gabe?" Paige whirled around. "Hey!"

Meggie caught her breath. *Wait a minute.* "Paige, what happened? Where'd he go?"

"He just disappeared."

But before Meggie could reply, a shadow moved out from the far right-hand corner of the porch. She grabbed Paige and felt the scream explode in her throat.

Long dark hair fell from the wide-brimmed hat. Black eyes caught the moon's reflection and hit Meggie like two black rocks.

The whipman.

Wool Barn

CHAPTER 14

Triple Trouble

"Eeeyoww!" Paige screamed, flying off the porch as though a jet-propelled engine had been stuck in her cutoffs.

Meggie followed, her sneakers, a white blur against the dust and weeds flying in every direction.

Paige led the way back to the campground, past creaky old shacks where shadows hovered and the night wind wailed. Terror kept them both moving at breakneck speed.

"Oooh, poor Gabe!" Paige cried out, the second they were inside the tent with the door zipped tight. "Poor Gabe!"

"And us!" Meggie added, her lips trembling. "We're not safe in this tent, Paige! Oh, where is Aunt Abby?"

"I don't know!" Paige cried, still clinging to her club. "Why isn't she back?"

Meggie wished she knew. She took off her glasses, wiping the sweat and dust off her cheeks and forehead. "What're we gonna do?"

"I don't know!" Paige was still gripping the club like it was their only hope.

"Paige, put the dumb club down. It's not going to help."

"It will if he tries to get in!"

Meggie whirled around and gazed out the screened window, her heart still thumping like a drum. Lights flashed against the tent. The van. Was it the van? Was Aunt Abby returning?

"Is it her?" Paige cried.

"I—I think so!"

"Thank heavens! But wait a minute, Meggie. What are we going to say? We promised Gabe we wouldn't tell!"

Meggie whirled around. "You promised him, Paige. I didn't."

Paige's chin fell. "Whoa, that's right."

"And he's in trouble. That whipman is hunting him down this very minute. We need to tell somebody. We have to help him whether he wants it or not! It's the right thing to do."

Paige nodded, turning back to the window and watched the headlights pull up beside the campsite.

Meggie and Paige burst out of the tent. "Aunt Abby!" Meggie cried, relief filling her words. "We're so glad you're back!"

"I'm sorry I'm so late," she said, taking off her hat and sitting down at the camp table. "We just got into this heavy discussion and before I knew it, time got away from me. And what's going on here? You two look like you just crawled out of an old barn."

"We did!" they exploded. "The wool barn!"

"You're not serious?" Her light tone changed as she sat down on the couch. "Why that's private property, girls. It's locked up. You two know better. And not at this late hour, especially."

"This kid helped us hide in there because the whipman was after us!" Paige told her.

"Ooops. Wait a minute. Who got you in there?" She brushed her frizz of hair from her eyes that had narrowed with concern.

"Gabe Stackpile!"

"StackPOLE," Meggie corrected. "Paige, let me tell her."

"Pole or a pile, it doesn't matter, Meggie!"

"Who is Gabe Stackpile?" Aunt Abby prodded.

"Remember Kilroy?" Paige said to her. "Remember the messages on the blackboard in the school and you thought it was Kilroy?"

"What's Kilroy got to do with this?" By this time Aunt Abby looked completely confused.

"Paige, we don't have much time. We have to drop Kilroy, Bluebeard, all that stuff. We have to tell Aunt Abby exactly what happened. Gabe's life depends on it!"

"I *know*, Meggie. I'm trying. You threw Bluebeard in, I didn't."

Aunt Abby got up and walked over to a thermos of coffee still on the table. "I think I need some nice, cold coffee," she said, shaking her head. "Maybe we can all sit down and I'll have my coffee and you have a soda, then we'll relax. We can talk about Kilroy and Bluebeard in the morning, okay?" She pulled out the coffeepot and removed the lid. "I think I've left you two girls alone a bit too long."

"No, you haven't! And it can't wait 'till morning!" Meggie pleaded, following her into the kitchen. "There's this guy named Gabe and it was him leaving those messages on the blackboard in the school. Remember we tried to tell you? Well, he's running away. He's in trouble, Aunt Abby. Right now he's out there in the wool barn and the whipman is after him. We have to help him!"

Aunt Abby poured her coffee, nearly spilling it. "What?" She spun around.

Meggie and Paige began to explain.

"Whipman?" Aunt Abby shook her head, getting more confused by the minute. "Did you say *whipman*?"

"Yes! And we even saw him with our own eyes! He's been following us!" Paige put in.

"He is *so* weird, Aunt Abby," Meggie added, throwing her hands around in a wild gesture. "He has this long, stringy black hair and these beady eyes that scared us to death!"

"And a stick that speaks to him? Girls..."

"Aunt Abby, you have to believe us," Meggie cried. "This time you have to listen and you have to believe us!"

"Okay, okay," she said, setting down her cup. "If he's a runaway then we can report that. My cellular phone isn't getting any service here, so we'll go over to the café and phone. If they're still open. Wait a minute..." She turned and stared at Meggie and Paige.

"What's wrong?" Paige asked, gripping the club tighter.

"A runaway from Warm Springs?"

"Yes!"

"At dinner somebody mentioned there's been a thirteen-year-old boy missing from the reservation. A runaway. Yes! Of course. This might be him!"

Meggie's hopes rose.

"Let's go!" she said, hurrying out the door. Her shirt flapped like a loose teepee in the night breeze.

When they reached the Café, Meggie's heart fell. Was it closed?

"Wait, I see Harriet cleaning up!" Paige called, running ahead. "Harriet!" she called, hurrying over to the door and banging on the glass. "Can we use the phone? It's an emergency!"

Harriet walked toward Paige with a frown on her face, but she unlocked the door.

"May we use the phone, Harriet?" Aunt Abby said to the woman. "We have to call the sheriff."

Meggie couldn't get Gabe off her mind, wondering if the whipman had found him. *Oh Gabe! Hang on! We're coming!*

In minutes her aunt had reached the sheriff and began giving him instructions. "Yes, yes. Well, the girls feel someone is pursuing him. They feel he's in danger so we're hoping you'll get down here right away."

"Tell them it's the whipman!" Paige told her, gesturing with her club.

"Paige, what is that? What's that terrible thing you have in your hand?" Aunt Abby said as soon as she hung up.

"A club. I made it myself."

"Yes, I can see that."

"If it wasn't for this club, we might be dead by now. There's more, Aunt Abby. We've been dealing with more than just a whipman."

"Really?" her aunt said, arching her brows and turning to Meggie.

"There is also a ghost *and* a Bushtn," Paige said.

Harriet rolled her eyeballs toward heaven and folded her arms. "Whipman? Ghost? Bushman? And served with catsup and french fries, no less? This is crazy. Crazy! But, I knew you two were up to something. I just knew it in my bones!"

"Huh?" Meggie turned to the waitress.

"Sneaking around like that. I knew something was going on. And I had a feeling it had something to do with that runaway too. I had a feeling you two were hiding him."

"It's a good thing we did," Paige told her, gripping her club tighter in her hand. "If it wasn't for us, he might be dead. We all might be dead. No telling what that stick might tell the whipman to do!"

"What stick?" Harriet gazed down at Meggie's club, looking confused again. A string of hair fell from her carefully groomed coif that had been sprayed and combed to perfection. She threw it back quickly, and turned to Abby.

"The Wasco County sheriff is on the way," Abby told her and the girls. "He was on Highway 97 when he got the call so the dispatcher said it shouldn't be long before he gets here."

Hurry, Meggie said silently, rushing over to the window and gazing out into the shadows of Shaniko where Gabe was hiding.

Please hurry.

CHAPTER 15

The Club

Before long, the brown and white vehicle pulled up in front of the Shaniko Hotel and Café, lights flashing.

"Tell the sheriff to turn off those lights!" Meggie said, hurrying out beside her aunt. "That's gonna scare Gabe away!"

"It's probably too late," Paige muttered, close on her heels. "If Gabe sees the sheriff, he's outta here. Zip. Gone."

In minutes the lights stopped flashing and the sheriff walked over to Meggie and Paige. At first he started writing everything down, but then he stopped.

"Whipman?" He adjusted his wide-brimmed Stetson hat and leaned forward. "Would you please repeat that?"

"Yes," Paige told him boldly. "Whipman. He's running away from the whipman. Not only that…"

"Paige," Meggie broke in, turning to her best friend. "Paige, the whipman is enough. For now. Know what I mean?"

Paige nodded. She understood.

The sheriff cleared his throat and turned to their aunt. "Uh, do you know about this—whipman thing?"

"Sir," Meggie interrupted, "Sir, we have to go there. Now. Somebody is following Gabe Stackpole and he's scared. He'll be scared of you too and we'll never find him if we just hang around here and talk!"

The sheriff finally agreed. They climbed into his vehicle and left Harriet standing in front of the restaurant shaking her head.

"He's probably hiding in the wool barn," Paige told the sheriff, pointing to the huge, rectangular shadow in the distance.

If he's still alive, Meggie thought grimly, buckling up as the sheriff pulled a U-turn and sped toward the old warehouse two blocks away.

"Or he might've split," Paige continued, brushing her hair from her wide eyes. "He was scared the whipman was gonna get him. We all were. Anyway, he might be half way to The Dalles or Bend by now."

In minutes they reached the wool barn. Darkness hovered like a giant bat with evil wings keening in the wind.

Gabe? Gabe, where are you? Meggie thought frantically, gazing around in the shadows. *It's okay. Everything's gonna be okay.*

Meggie watched the sheriff get out of the vehicle and climb over the fence, his tan and brown uniform blending into the shadows. She listened to him call out in the darkness and knew that if Gabe was in the building, he'd hear.

"Gabe? Gabe Stackpole?" he called out, shining his flashlight around. "We're here to help. The girls explained everything. It's all right now. Everything's going to be fine." He moved slowly, cautiously, toward the dilapidated porch.

But there was no answer. Nothing but the wind crawling over the grass and up the walls of the old structure. Nothing but her heartbeat thumping likes a wild drum inside her shirt.

Aunt Abby stepped out of the car, her oversized shirt quivering in the wind. "Maybe we can help?" she called to the sheriff who was shining his light around and tugging at the locked doors.

Meggie and Paige followed her, leaning against the fence.

"Gabe? Gabe, it's me, Meggie!"

"And me, Paige!"

Still no answer. Nothing.

"We had to do this, Gabe! We had to help you!" Meggie went on, raising her voice, hoping he could hear. Hoping he was still here.

"Yeah!" Paige called out. "Plus, I've still got my club!"

The sheriff turned and gazed down at the thing in her hand, then up at their aunt.

Abby shrugged, dusting off her trousers. And they waited. The minutes felt like hours and still there was nothing. Only the creaking and moaning of the wind in the old warehouse gave answer. *Is it laughing?* Meggie wondered as she gazed around in the bleak shadows. *And is he laughing too? Is the whipman in there laughing at all of us?* She cringed.

"He might be in this tunnel at the other end of the building," Meggie told the sheriff finally.

"Yeah," Page put in. "It leads to this room that's closed off except for the trap doors. The one overhead takes you across the rafters and brings you here to this end."

Meggie nodded. "When we knew the whipman was following us, Gabe showed us all these secret tunnels and stuff. And this place is huge. I guess he could be just about anywhere."

"I think we're going to need to wait for the Warm Springs tribal police to get here," the sheriff said, returning and motioning them back into his vehicle. "I contacted them when I got your call. It doesn't appear the boy is going to cooperate. He's just not coming out."

"Well maybe that's because he's not in there," Paige said.

If he's not in there, then did he get away in time? Meggie wondered. *But even if they bring in a posse or the Swat Team, can they track him down in time? Gabe knows how to hide. He knows how to slip in and out of tunnels and doors and practically disappear.* She and Paige had found that out, hadn't they?

"I'll take you back to the hotel to wait until the tribal police get here," the sheriff told them. "This boy is under their jurisdiction."

"We can't just leave him here with th—that..." Meggie couldn't finish. The words were jammed up in her throat.

"That monster!" Paige blurted, gripping her club. "We won't leave Gabe! We can't!"

But Meggie knew they didn't have a choice. The way Aunt Abby looked them straight in the eye told them both they were to do exactly as they were told. Exactly.

Back in the hotel lobby, people were practically coming out of the wallpaper.

"What's going on, honey?" an elderly lady with blue hair asked Meggie.

"Uh—well..." Meggie didn't know what to say.

"It's the runaway from the Warm Springs Reservation, Ethel," Miss Knepper, the hotel manager said. "The girls spotted him in the warehouse."

"And the school," Paige put in.

"The school?" Harriet's words hit like rocks from the doorway behind them. She turned to Paige and frowned. "So you *were* in the school, weren't you?"

"Following the ghost," Paige said with a nod.

"Ghost?" The elderly woman nearly fell backwards over a faded settee. "Oh my, how exciting! I absolutely adore hearing about ghosts!"

That's not all," Paige went on. "We also..."

"Paige, we better stop."

"Yeah?"

"Oh no, dears, don't stop, please. This is the most excitement I've had in years!" The old woman was practically dancing. By this time people began to gather around.

But Harriet wasn't excited. Even though Meggie realized they hadn't really done anything wrong, she could tell Harriet still didn't like them snooping around Shaniko.

If it weren't for us, Gabe might still be eating out of the garbage bin behind the hotel this very minute, Meggie wanted to tell her. And yet, maybe that would've been better than the mess he was in now. But wouldn't the whipman find him sooner or later? *At least now he has a chance.*

"The window right over the cellar roof wasn't even boarded up," Paige said to the lady. "We just heard these howling noises and went in to check it out."

"Oooh, how exciting!" The old woman rushed forward, catching her flowered polyester dress on a chair and sending the chair flying. "I knew this place was going to be the vacation of a lifetime, Lois," she called back to her elderly sister. "I just knew it!"

Fortunately Aunt Abby walked in with some sandwiches at exactly the right moment.

"Would you like one too?" she asked the lady with the blue hair who was practically sitting on Paige's lap by now.

"Oh no, thank you dear. I've just had my prunes."

"Well girls," Aunt Abby said. "The tribal police should be here any time now. Let's go outside and wait."

Meggie drew a sigh of relief and told the nice elderly lady they'd probably see her later. The woman's face fell. She seemed disappointed—as though all of a sudden her vacation had been ruined. Meggie thought she was going to cry.

"Here, you can have this," Paige said, handing her the club.

"What is it, dear?" Crinkly eyes widened with hope.

"A club. It's fantastic if you're going after ghosts."

"Paige…" Meggie turned and watched her best friend give the dorky club to the lady.

"I'm honored. Thrilled!" The woman almost fell over again.

"I'll miss that club," Paige told Meggie as soon as they were outside on the porch. "I really will. But we probably don't need it anymore."

"*Paige.*"

Paige shrugged and sat down on the whiskey barrel.

In the distance Meggie saw the headlights. It looked like two—no three more cars. Yes, help was on the way. The Warm Springs tribal police were coming. But it had taken them almost an hour.

Was it too late?

CHAPTER 16

Closing In

"Our men are going to circle the building and go inside," the Warm Springs police sergeant said, taking some keys from Miss Knepper as well as a map of the layout of the warehouse. "Thanks for your help, M'am, and thank the owner of the building for his cooperation. We didn't want to have to get a search warrant and break in if we didn't have to."

After the sergeant consulted with the Wasco County sheriff and gave everyone their instructions, he turned to Meggie and Paige.

"Since you are his friends, we may need you. You and your aunt can follow us in your vehicle, but we ask that you stay inside your car and keep your doors locked until we know everything will be safe. We've also notified his family and they should be here shortly."

Meggie felt a rush of relief. *At least he believes us.*

"Safe?" Paige whispered to Meggie as soon as they were inside the van and heading toward the wool barn. "He'll never come out if *she's* there."

"Who?"

"His evil stepmother," Paige told Meggie. "She's on the way. You heard the sergeant."

Meggie hadn't thought about that. They didn't have enough time to tell the police all the details—like the stepmother putting the whipping stick above Gabe's door. But, since the sheriff seemed to be having trouble with the basics like the whipman, the tribal police might really freak out if she and Paige started talking about a stick that gave messages.

And what had Gabe done that was so bad? she wondered. Then there was the Bushtn. Thank goodness Paige didn't bring up the Bushtn. Meggie wrapped her arms around her slender frame and shivered in the back seat, gazing around in the pale light as they drove up and parked near the gate. *Please be okay, Gabe. Please.*

One of the officers unlocked the gate and started toward the old building.

"Gabe? Gabe Stackpole?" The officer said over a loudspeaker. "This is Sergeant Scott from Warm Springs and we want you to know we're here to help you. Your friends told us everything and you don't need to be afraid."

"Maybe we should've told them everything," Paige whispered, frowning. "If they knew *everything*..."

"Shhh!" Meggie whispered, rolling down the window so that she could hear better.

"Gabe, our officers are surrounding the building and we intend to apprehend anyone who might be attempting to hurt you. You're safe. You can come out and nothing will happen. Your parents are on the way."

"Parents! Oh no!" Paige threw up her hands in despair. "That's gonna blow it, Meggie. That's gonna blow the whole thing!"

"Shhh!" Aunt Abby said.

Meggie knew Paige might be right. She wished they'd told the tribal police about his evil stepmother. But it was too late. She pushed the hopeless thoughts aside and gazed out the window into the darkness, watching. Listening.

"Gabe Stackpole?" The loud voice boomed out into the darkness once again. "We're coming in. We're coming into the warehouse now. We won't hurt you. Please know we just want to help you."

Oh Gabe...are you even there? Or did you run? Did you get away in time? Did you take off to nowhere? Meggie waited, her thoughts darting recklessly, hopelessly, like the scudding clouds overhead. Time dragged and there was nothing. Nothing.

But what could they do? Then suddenly it hit Meggie. Yes, wait a minute. Maybe there *was* something she and Paige could do. Sure, why not? *Why not?*

"What's taking them so long?" Paige cut into Meggie's thoughts, her voice as taut as a fence wire.

Aunt Abby shook her head. "He must have found a pretty good place to hide, that's all I've got to say."

"Yeah," Paige agreed. "Not only that, he knows how to keep moving so they'll never find him. Never."

"But if he's still in there, then I want to talk to him, Aunt Abby," Meggie said finally. "I want to try and talk him into coming out."

Paige faced her, wide-eyed.

"If the police let us, will you help me, Paige? We can talk just like we did in the school. Like friends, y'know?"

Paige nodded.

"Will you ask him, Aunt Abby?" Meggie went on. "Will you go out and ask the tribal police if we can talk to Gabe over that loudspeaker?"

Her aunt drew a deep breath and nodded. "Well, I don't see why not. It couldn't hurt, certainly." She flashed the headlights and stepped out of the van.

In a few moments, the officer in charge nodded and motioned the girls out of the vehicle.

Meggie walked over and took the loudspeaker from his hand. She tried to hold her hands steady so they wouldn't wobble like her knees. "Gabe? Gabe, it's me, Meggie! Meggie Bryson. See—we had to help you so that's why we got the sheriff."

"Yeah," Paige blurted, leaning into the cone-shaped voice box. "These guys will deck that..."

"Uh, Gabe?" Meggie drew the mouthpiece away from Paige, her hands still shaking. "If you come out, we'll all talk and explain what's going on and stuff. We won't let anything happen to you. Nothing."

"You have our word, Gabe Stackpile!" Paige blurted, swinging her fist.

"Paige."

Then suddenly, Meggie heard a sound. She whirled around. Headlights. A car. *Oh no.* Was it Gabe's folks? Her throat tightened.

Sergeant Scott took the loudspeaker from her hand and thanked them both. "This may be his parents," he said, walking toward the gate.

"Now he'll *never* come out!" Paige wailed.

Meggie knew Paige might be right. She braced herself against the fence and watched as the car slowed down and pulled in. A man got out.

"I'm Charlie Stackpole," he said, reaching out to shake the officer's hand. "And this is Rose, my wife, and Bobby, our son."

"She doesn't look evil to me," Meggie whispered to Paige. The woman had short, dark hair sprinkled with gray and eyes that looked scared.

Paige snorted. "She's probably hiding it. That's what they do."

Meggie swallowed hard, watching them talk to the officers. "His dad looks like he's okay, though, don't you think? And I didn't know Gabe had a little brother."

"Neither did I."

The kid didn't look a thing like Gabe. The pudgy cheeks and cowlick reminded Meggie of an eight-year-old Dennis the Menace with dark hair and eyes.

Suddenly, Meggie saw something out of the corner of her eye. She turned and threw her hand over her mouth, stifling a scream.

A shadow stepped out from behind the wool barn and started coming toward them. Terror gripped her by the throat. *It's him.*

The whipman.

CHAPTER 17

Defective Detective

Stringy hair beneath the wide-brimmed hat caught the wind as the lanky form walked toward them. The black eyes pierced like bullets.

"You're under arrest!" Paige screamed, backing up to Sergeant Scott. "Stop! Stop!"

"Do something!" Meggie blurted, the minute she could breathe. "It's him! He's the one who's been following us!"

"Whoa—hold it," the Warm Springs police officer said to Paige and Meggie.

The man moved closer, leather-clad trousers rustling in the sudden, bizarre silence. "I'm Detective Hayes with the Warm Springs tribal police," he said. He reached for his badge.

"Hah! That is no Defective!" Paige exploded.

"Paige, wait." Aunt Abby grabbed her arm.

Meggie felt her throat go dry. *Detective? Oh no.*

"It's the whipman!" Paige blurted again, her eyes filled with anger. She was standing her ground. "This is the sleaze-ball who's been fol-

96

lowing us all over Shaniko!"

The dark stranger held out his badge. "I've been following you, yes," he said to Paige, then to Meggie. "I suspected you knew where the runaway was hiding out. And I do apologize if my—uh, my appearance is a bit unconventional. It's part of the job. Undercover work."

I can't believe this. I can't. So he isn't the whipman after all. Meggie was stunned. Speechless.

Suddenly, Gabe came bursting out of the wool barn, racing down the steps toward them. "Let them go!" he yelled, running toward the slim, spider-like shadow of the stranger. Gabe's eyes were wild, his voice hard.

"It's okay, Gabe!" Meggie ran toward him. "He's not the whipman! He's not!"

Gabe skidded to a halt, dust flying.

"He's a detective!" Paige told him, running up behind Meggie.

"A whaat?" Gabe's head darted around, his dark hair falling in his face with each jerk.

"He's an undercover detective," Gabe's father said, walking toward him. "We—we needed help finding you, Son."

"No." Gabe backed up.

"Gabe, I…" his dad struggled for words, "why did you feel you had to leave us?"

The sergeant stepped back, motioning for the assisting officers to do the same.

Gabe dropped his gaze, then looked up and turned to Meggie and Paige. "You're okay, then?"

They both nodded.

"I thought…"

"I know," Meggie said, swallowing hard. "And thanks. I mean, you risked a lot coming out here like that to—to..."

"To save you from the cop, right?" A lopsided smile slid up one side of Gabe's face, then disappeared.

"Gabe?" It was his father again.

Gabe turned and faced his dad.

"What happened, Son? Why? What can we do?" His father held his gaze.

"Get rid of her!" Paige blurted. "Get rid of his evil stepmother!"

"Paige!" Aunt Abby cried, aghast.

Gabe stood rigid. His eyes flashing. His chin firm.

"Evil?" Gabe's father turned as his wife and son walked up from behind.

"Yes, evil! Wicked!" Paige went on. "She put the whipping stick up over his bedroom door so that the whipman would come. She wanted to punish him! She's terrible!"

"Paige, stop." Aunt Abby grabbed her arm, turning to the floundering woman in apology.

"I did it!" the pudgy little brother blurted. "It was me! I put that stick up there!"

Everyone turned and stared at Bobby Stackpole.

"I did it on account of what he stole," he whined. The rumpled-haired Dennis the Menace turned to his older brother. His eyes watered up. "I knew what you did, Gabe. I knew what you were hiding back in the woods. I was just playing a trick, y'know? I didn't think you'd take off like that."

Gabe's shoulders fell, but he still couldn't look his stepmother in the eye. "You little dork," he said to his brother finally.

"Sorry, Gabe."

"I'm sorry too, Gabe," his stepmother said, walking up to him. "I'm talking about the rest of what happened. I felt so bad about what I'd done, but when I went back..."

But before she could finish her sentence, a familiar, eerie howl split the darkness behind them, sending chills straight down Meggie's back. She whirled around, petrified.

"Eeeeyow!" Paige shrieked. "The ghost!"

Dumbstruck, Meggie stared at the pale white thing howling underneath the moon. *A dog! A little white dog!* She almost fell over in shock. "Whaaat...?"

Gabe ran across the bunchgrass toward the dog. "You keep gettin' me in trouble, Bushtn!" He picked up the hound and held it close.

Bushtn? Meggie turned to Paige whose chin had dropped a mile.

"Whoa! You mean—that's the ghost? *And* the Bushtn?" Paige asked, shaking her head in complete amazement. "Oh, my gosh, Meggie. Can you believe this? *Can you believe this?*"

Meggie watched Gabe walk toward them, the little white dog in his arms. No, she couldn't. This was unreal. *Unreal.* "Then, it was *you?*" Meggie said finally, remembering the howling coming from the tower in the schoolhouse. "You were hiding him back at the school, too, weren't you? And in the warehouse. Gabe, you scared us to death!"

He nodded with a guilty shrug.

"I felt terrible when I went to get your dog back from those people, because when I got there, it was gone," Gabe's stepmother said from behind, walking toward her stepson. "They said one of their children must have left the gate open. My heart was sick."

Meggie and Paige turned to the woman who had tears in her voice now. "It was hard enough for you having a brand new stepmother, but when I wasn't willing to keep the dog—your dog—well, that was just too much to ask and I knew it, Gabe. But when I went back to get your dog, it was too late. I didn't know what to do and then a few days later you ran off."

A lingering silence hung heavy.

"Yeah, well it was me who left that gate open. I took him," Gabe said, still holding his little hound close. "I didn't know how much longer I could keep him hid though, and then when I saw that stick over my door, I..."

"He was hiding Bushtn in the woods out back," his Dennis the Menace brother told the woman. "I thought for sure you were gonna hear it howling, too."

"So that was it? That was the bad thing you did, Gabe?" It was Meggie now.

He nodded, holding his little dog closer. Two huge brown eyes were gazing up into Gabe's face and a long tail was swinging like a barn rope below his arm.

"I'm sorry, Gabe," Rose Stackpole said, reaching out and petting the little hound. "But I'm so glad he's back. I'm glad you're back."

"I owe you an apology too, Son," his father put in, placing an arm around his shoulder. "I think I've learned some things, as well."

"Yeah, me too," his little brother added with a lame smile. "That dumb stick..."

Gabe looked at his father and nodded, then dropped his head into Bushtn's fur and nuzzled him gently. "I, uh—I didn't know you'd gone back—to get him," he said to his new stepmother.

"I'm really glad about that, too," Paige put in. "I mean, gee, you're not wicked or evil at all. In fact you're really nice."

Meggie swallowed hard, smiling at Paige.

And Gabe was smiling too.

"Well, shall we take Bushtn back to Warm Springs Gabe?" Charlie Stackpole said.

Gabe nodded, then turned to Meggie and Paige. "Uh—thanks," he said to them both. "Thanks a lot."

"It was nothin," Paige said with a shrug.

But Meggie couldn't say one single thing. The words were all jammed up in her throat. She and Paige watched in silence as Gabe walked toward the car.

Then he paused and turned to Meggie and Paige, the familiar lop-sided grin moving up one side of his face. "Pretty cool, Bushtns," he said to them both. "Pretty cool, huh?"

And then he was gone.

Gabe Stackpole and his little white dog got into the car with his family and went back home to Warm Springs.

CHAPTER 18

Goodbye Shaniko

Meggie and Paige knew they were going to be driving past the old school on their way out of Shaniko.

The old Shaniko school where everything began.

The ghost.

The Bushtn.

The whipman.

"Well," Paige said to Meggie as the van pulled the trailer out of the campsite, "at least we weren't completely off track." She sat in the far back with her best friend, gazing out the window. "I mean, hey, there really is such a thing as a whipman."

"I know" Meggie said, shaking her head.

"And a *whiplady!* Can you believe Warm Springs used to have a whiplady too?"

Meggie nodded. "It's a good thing they don't do stuff like that very much anymore," she said.

"Well, if it was me and I had to make a choice, then, I'd choose the whiplady over the whipman, wouldn't you, Meggie?"

The van hit a rut as it passed the Shaniko Hotel and Café. "I wouldn't want either one," she said to Paige.

"At least that's not gonna happen to Gabe. And I'm glad, Meggie. I'm really glad everything's turning out right for him. Mostly though, I'm glad he's got his little dog back."

"Yeah. Me too."

"Funny name, though, huh?"

Meggie turned to Paige.

"Bushtn. A weird name for a dog, don't you think?"

"Yeah, I guess."

"And he called us Bushtns, too, Meggie. Remember in the school? Then in the warehouse? I wasn't really sure, but when he said goodbye—he said it again, remember? How come he called us Bushtns?"

Meggie's thoughts backed up. Paige was right. He had called them Bushtns, hadn't he? She remembered that first night in the school and then again tonight when he was walking away with his folks, saying goodbye.

"Pretty cool, Bushtns. Pretty cool, huh..."

"Bushtn is a Wasco word," Aunt Abby called over her shoulder from the driver's seat. "It's an Indian word meaning 'white man.'"

Meggie turned to Paige. "White man?"

"You think that could also mean white lady?" Paige said to her. "White lady. White dog. Hey, Meggie—it could even mean white girl, don't you think?"

"I guess."

"Except I'm not white." Paige held out her sun-bronzed arm and turned to her best friend. "I'll bet anything I've got as good a tan as he has. Except we'll never know, will we? It was always so dark."

"I guess we won't," Meggie replied, knowing she'd never forget Gabe Stackpole. "It doesn't matter, though, does it, Paige? The color never made a difference."

"I know."

Then suddenly the van hit another rut. Meggie looked up. They were passing the Shaniko School.

"Meggie!" Paige blurted, pointing toward the school. "Look!"

Meggie turned and gazed at the steepled, weather-beaten structure beaming proudly in the full blaze of the morning sun.

There on the cellar roof was the little lady with the blue hair, her polyester dress fluttering like a flag in the wind. She was clutching Paige's club in one hand, struggling to get inside the small window.

"Will you look at *that?*" Paige gasped, exploding into laughter.

"Pretty cool, Bushtn," Meggie said to her best friend. "Pretty cool, huh?"

AUTHOR'S NOTE

The idea for the story was triggered by a newspaper article about a Warm Springs tribal whipping. Though seldom used today, the public punishment employed by the Whipman still occurs on some reservations in order to make discipline a community concern.

How to Order Books by Calamity Jan

BILL TO:

NAME

ADDRESS

CITY   STATE   ZIP

SHIP TO:

NAME

ADDRESS

CITY   STATE   ZIP

PRODUCT	COST	QTY	TOTAL
Goodbye God, I'm Going to Bodie (ISBN 0-9721800-0-1)	$10.00		
Ghost of Nighthawk (ISBN 0-9721800-1-x)	$10.00		
Shadow of Shaniko (ISBN 0-9721800-2-8)	$10.00		

SHIPPING RATES: Add $2.50 for first copy, $.75 each additional book.	SHIPPING
	TAX Washington State residents, add 8% sales tax.
BOOKSTORE/LIBRARY/WHOLESALE ORDERS: Orders of 10 or more books, apply standard 40% discount. S&Handling rates (above) apply.	**TOTAL**

Please allow 4 to 6 weeks for US delivery.

Prices are subject to change without notice.

Visit www.CalamityJan.com or check out
http://www.booksinprint.com/php/phpFeaturedTitle.asp?WildWest_Publishing